**Maximo placed his hand over her stomach again, his expression intense. "This is my baby that you carry, Alison. Our baby. I could not feel it more if you had conceived in my bed."**

His accent was thicker than she'd ever heard it, his voice a husky rasp that made her nipples tighten and her pulse pound.

"The attraction between us is very convenient."

"Convenient?" Her tongue felt thick and clumsy, her mind still clouded by passion.

"Of course. How could it not be convenient for me to feel desire for my future wife?"

## All about the author...
### *Maisey Yates*

**MAISEY YATES** knew she wanted to be a writer, even before she knew what it was she wanted to write.

At her very first job she was fortunate enough to meet her very own tall, dark and handsome hero, who happened to be her boss, and promptly married him and started a family. It wasn't until she was pregnant with her second child that she found her very first Harlequin Presents® books in a local thrift store. By the time she'd reached the happily ever after, she had fallen in love. She devoured as many as she could get her hands on after that, and she knew that these were the books she wanted to write!

She started submitting, and nearly two years later, while pregnant with her third child, she received The Call from her editor. At the age of twenty-three she sold her first manuscript to Harlequin Presents®, and she was very glad that the good news didn't send her into labor!

She still can't quite believe she's blessed enough to see her name on not just any book, but her favorite books.

Maisey lives with her supportive, handsome, wonderful, diaper-changing husband and three small children across the street from her parents and the home she grew up in, in the wilds of southern Oregon. She enjoys living in a place where you might wake up to find a bear on your back porch and then head into the home office to write stories that take place in exotic, urban locales.

# Maisey Yates

## AN ACCIDENTAL
## BIRTHRIGHT

TORONTO NEW YORK LONDON
AMSTERDAM PARIS SYDNEY HAMBURG
STOCKHOLM ATHENS TOKYO MILAN MADRID
PRAGUE WARSAW BUDAPEST AUCKLAND

Recycling programs
for this product may
not exist in your area.

ISBN-13: 978-0-373-12985-0

AN ACCIDENTAL BIRTHRIGHT

Previously published in the U.K. as
A MISTAKE, A PRINCE AND A PREGNANCY

First North American Publication 2011

Copyright © 2010 by Maisey Yates

# AN ACCIDENTAL
# BIRTHRIGHT

# CHAPTER ONE

"OH, PLEASE don't rebel on me now." Alison Whitman put her hand over her stomach and tried to quell the rising nausea that was threatening her with immediate action if she didn't get a hold of some saltine crackers or a bottle of ginger ale. Morning sickness was the pits, and it was even worse when it lasted all day. Worse still when you were about to tell a man he was going to be a father.

Alison put her car in Park and took a deep breath, almost relieved to discover a roadblock in her path. The wrought-iron gates that partitioned the massive mansion from the rest of the world looked impenetrable. She didn't know a lot about this man, the father of her baby; nothing really other than his name. But it was clear that he was way out of her league, both financially and otherwise.

Her eyes widened when she saw a man in a dark suit with security-issue sunglasses prowling the perimeter of the fence. Was Max Rossi mafia or something? Who had security detail in the middle of nowhere in Washington State?

The guard, because that's what he had to be, exited through a smaller pedestrian gate and walked toward her car, his expression grim. He gestured for her to roll her window down and she complied, self-conscious of the crank handle that she had to use to perform the action. Her car wasn't exactly a new, fully loaded model.

"Are you lost, ma'am?" He sounded perfectly pleasant and polite, but she knew that his right hand, which looked as though it was resting on his hip and was partly concealed by his dark suit jacket, was likely gripping a gun.

"No. I'm looking for Mr. Rossi. This is the address I was given."

The man's lips turned up slightly. "Sorry. Mr. Rossi isn't receiving visitors."

"I'm…" She swallowed. "I'm Alison Whitman. He's expecting me. At least I think he is."

The guard held up a hand, pulled a cell phone from his pocket and hit Speed Dial. He spoke rapidly in a foreign language, Italian, she guessed, before hanging up and turning his attention back to her.

"Go ahead and pull in. Park your car at the front." He walked to the gate and keyed in a code. The iron monstrosities swung forward and Alison pulled the car through, her stomach now seriously protesting.

She really didn't know Max Rossi; she had no assurance he wouldn't harm her in some way. Maybe she hadn't thought this through.

No, that wasn't true. She *had* thought this through. From every angle until she was certain she had no choice but to come here and see the father of her baby, despite the fact that she wanted to bury her head in a hole and pretend the whole thing had never happened. She couldn't play ostrich on this one, no matter how much she might like to.

The house was massive, its bulk partially concealed by towering fir trees. The intensity of the saturated greens surrounding her was almost surreal, compliments of the year-round rainfall. Nothing new to a native of the Pacific Northwest, but she rarely ventured outside the Seattle city limits anymore, so being surrounded by this much nature felt like a new experience. And seeing such a pristine, modern mansion set in the middle of the rugged wilderness was akin to an out-of-body experience.

Of course, the past two weeks had also seemed like an out-of-body experience; first with the positive pregnancy test, and then with all of the revelations that had followed.

She parked her ancient car in front of the house and got out slowly, really hoping she didn't lose her lunch in the middle of the paved driveway. Not exactly a way to make a good impression on a man.

The security detail appeared out of nowhere, his hand clamping firmly on her arm as he led her to the front door.

"I appreciate the chivalrous gesture, but I can make it through the door on my own," she said drily.

Her escort gave her a rueful smile, but loosened his grip and let his hand fall to his side. Although she noticed he was still ready to grab hold of her if he needed to.

He opened the front door for her and she had a feeling it wasn't good manners that made him allow her to go in first, but a desire to keep himself in the most advantageous position.

"Ms. Whitman." The deep, velvet voice held just a hint of an accent and the sound made her already queasy stomach turn, but not with nausea. This feeling was something she didn't recognize at all; a strange twisting sensation that wasn't entirely unpleasant. She put a hand to her stomach and tried to suppress it.

The sight of the owner of the amazing voice only increased the pitching sensation. She watched as he strode down the sweeping, curved staircase, his movements quick and smooth, masculine yet graceful.

He was the most handsome man she'd ever seen— not that she ever spent much time dwelling on men and their looks. This man, though, demanded admiration, even from her. He was just so masculine, so striking. He would turn both male and female heads wherever he went, that was for sure. And not just because of his arresting features and perfect physique. It was his air of authority, the absolute power that emanated from him. It was compelling in a way that captivated her.

His square jaw was set and uncompromising. Hard eyes, dark and fathomless, framed by a fringe of thick eyelashes, stared down at her. If not for the expression in his eyes, she might have called them beautiful, but the intense glare that he fixed on her put paid to that description.

He looked familiar, although she couldn't imagine where she would have ever seen someone like him. Such an example of masculine perfection hardly haunted the halls of the pro bono law firm where she worked.

She swallowed thickly and took a deep breath, hoping the infusion of fresh air would banish some of the nausea she felt. "Yes."

"You're from the clinic?" he asked, coming to a stop in front of her. His posture would make a marine envious. She had to crane her neck to look at him, his height topping her own five foot four inches by at least a foot.

"Yes…no. Not exactly. I don't know how much

Melissa explained when she called you." Melissa was one of her dearest friends in the world, and when she'd heard about the mistake made at the clinic she'd not only contacted Alison right away with Max's information—against the wishes of her boss—but she'd offered to be the one to contact Max, as well.

"Not a lot, only that it was an urgent matter. Which it had better be."

Not for the first time she contemplated just turning around and leaving, leaving the whole situation behind her. But that was the coward's way out. She didn't believe in leaving loose ends, and, unlike some other people, she didn't walk away from her responsibilities. Not ever.

"Is there somewhere we can go and speak privately?" she asked, looking around the cavernous entryway. No doubt the house had a lot of private rooms where they could sit and talk. Of course, the idea of being in an enclosed space with a man she'd never met didn't rank as a favorite for her. She was trained in self-defense and she had pepper spray on her key chain, but that didn't mean she wanted to get in a situation where she would have to use either one. Especially since she had a feeling neither one would prove effective against Max Rossi.

"I don't have a lot of time, Ms. Whitman."

Anger flared through her. *He* didn't have a lot of time? As if she had any spare moments just lying around. It was difficult for her to take any time off of work. Every case they handled was vitally important to the people involved. They were advocating for those who couldn't advocate for themselves, and by taking the afternoon off to drive up here and talk to him she was leaving her clients in the lurch.

"I can assure you that my time is valuable, too,

Mr. Rossi," she said stiffly. "But I need to speak with you."

"Then speak," he said.

"I'm pregnant," she said, wishing, even as she said the words, that she could call them back.

A muscle in his jaw ticked. "Am I meant to offer congratulations?"

"You're the father."

His dark eyes hardened. "You and I both know that isn't possible. You may not keep a record of your lovers, Ms. Whitman, but I can assure you I'm not so promiscuous that I forget mine."

Her face heated. "There are other ways to conceive a child than sexual intercourse, as you well know. When Melissa from ZoiLabs called she implied that I worked there but I'm a...I'm a client of theirs."

He froze, his expression hardening like granite, his jaw tightening. "Let's go into my office."

She followed him through the large living area of the house and through a heavy oak door. His home office was massive, with high ceilings that were accented by rich, natural wood beams. One of the walls was made entirely of glass and overlooked the valley below. There was nothing as far as she could see but pristine nature. Beautiful. But the view was cold comfort in the situation.

"There was a mistake at the clinic," she said, keeping her eyes trained on the mountains in the distance. "They weren't going to tell me, but one of my friends works there and she felt I...that I had a right to know. I was given your donation by mistake and there was no log of your...of your genetic testing."

"How is this possible?" he asked, pacing the room with long strides.

"I wasn't offered a specific explanation. The nearest thing to an answer I got is that your sample was mixed up with the donor I had selected because your last names were similar. My intended donor was a Mr. Ross."

Max gave her a hard look. "He was not your husband or boyfriend?"

"I don't have a husband or a boyfriend. It was all meant to be done anonymously. But…" She took a shaky breath. "It isn't that simple now."

His lip curled. "Not so simple now that you've found out the 'donor' for your child is a wealthy man? Are you here to collect some kind of prenatal child support?"

Alison bristled. "That isn't it at all! I'm sorry to have bothered you, I really am. I'm sure you didn't expect the recipient of your donation to show up on your doorstep. But I need to know if you underwent genetic testing prior to using the clinic."

"I didn't leave a donation," he said, his voice rough.

"You must have! She gave me your name. She said it was your sperm that was given to me by mistake."

A muscle in his jaw tightened and she noticed him slowly squeezing his hands into fists and releasing them, as if in attempt to gain control over his temper. "I had a sperm sample at the clinic, but it was not meant for anonymous donation. It was for my wife. We were having trouble conceiving."

"Oh." Alison felt all of the blood drain from her face, leaving her light-headed and dizzy. Now she really wanted to turn and run away. She'd read horror stories in the paper about couples involved in mix-ups, and people losing their babies. She clamped a possessive hand over her stomach. The baby was still hers, even if this man was the biological father. She was still the mother. No judge would take a baby from a competent, loving mother. And Max's wife wouldn't want a baby that didn't belong to her anyway. She couldn't.

"I just…I just need to know…" She took a breath. "I'm a nonaffected carrier of Cystic Fibrosis. The donors are all screened for genetic disorders before they're accepted. But your results weren't in the file. Melissa knew that I was concerned and she was going to get me the information about you, only it wasn't there."

"That's because I wasn't a *donor*," he said harshly.

"But have you been tested?" she asked, desperation clawing at her. She had to know. Watching her sister succumb to the disease in childhood had been the hardest thing Alison had ever endured. It had been the end of everything. Her family, her happiness. She had to know so that she could prepare herself for the worst. She wouldn't terminate her pregnancy. No matter what, she wouldn't do that. The memory of her sister, of that wonderful, short life, was far too dear to her to consider that. But she *did* need to know.

"I have not had that test done."

She sank into the plush chair that was positioned in front of the desk, her knees unable to support her anymore. "You need to get it done," she said. "*Please. I need you to do it.*"

Maximo examined the woman sitting in front of him, his heart pounding heavily in his chest. He hadn't given a thought to the clinic in the past two years, not since Selena's death. When he'd received the phone call from the employee at ZoiLabs he had assumed it pertained to his sperm sample. They had called shortly after the accident to ask him if they could discard it, but he'd ignored the voice mail message. At the time he simply hadn't been able to deal with it. He hadn't imagined that these might be the consequences.

Now he was going to be a father. It was the most amazing and terrifying moment he'd ever experienced. His gaze dropped to Alison's flat stomach. She was so slender it was almost impossible to believe that she could be carrying his baby. *His* baby. A son or daughter.

He could easily see a vision of a dark-haired child, cradled in Alison Whitman's arms as she looked down at the infant with a small, maternal smile on her face. The image filled him with longing so intense that his chest ached with it. He thought that he'd let that desire go, the desire for children. He thought he'd laid that dream to rest, alongside his wife.

But in one surreal moment all of those dreams had been made possible again. And in that very same moment he'd found out that his child might have serious health complications. His tightly controlled life was suddenly, definitely, out of his control. Everything that had seemed important five minutes ago was insignificant now, and everything that mattered to him rested in the womb of this stranger.

But he could get the test. Find out as soon as possible if there was a chance their baby might have the disease. Having something to do, something to hold on to, real action that he could take, helped anchor the whole situation to reality, allowed him to have some control back. It made it easier to believe that there really was a baby.

"I will have the test done right away," he said. He hadn't been planning on going back to Turan for another two weeks, but this took precedence. He would need to see his personal physician at the palace. He wouldn't take any chances on having this made a spectacle by the press. They'd caused enough damage in his life. "And what are you planning if the test is positive?"

She looked down at her hands. They were delicate,

feminine hands, void of jewelry and nail polish. It was far too easy to imagine how soft those hands would feel on his body, how pale they would look against the dark skin of his chest. A pang of lust hit him low in the gut. She was a beautiful woman; there was no denying that. Much less adorned than the type of woman he was accustomed to.

Her face had only the bare minimum of makeup, showing flawless ivory skin, her copper eyes left unenhanced by colored eyeshadow. Her full lips had just a bit of pale pink gloss on them that wouldn't take long to kiss right off.

Her strawberry blond hair was straight, falling well past her shoulders, and it looked as if it would be soft to touch, not stiff with product. A man would be able to sift it through his fingers and watch it spill over his pillow. His stomach tightened further. It said a lot about how much neglect his libido had endured if he was capable of being aroused at this precise moment. And when had a woman ever appealed to him so immediately? When had lust grabbed him so hard? Never in his recent memory, that was certain. Guilt, usually easy to ignore after living with it for so long, gnawed at him, harder and more insistent than usual.

"I'm keeping the baby no matter what," she said slowly, raising her eyes to meet his. "I just need to be prepared."

Something about the way she said that *she* was keeping the baby, as if he, the child's father, had no place in its life, caused a torrent of hot, possessive anger to flood through him. It was so intense that it momentarily blotted out the lust that had just been firing through his veins.

"The baby isn't yours. The baby is ours," he said.

"But…but you and your wife…"

He froze, realizing suddenly that she didn't know who he was. It didn't seem possible. Her face betrayed nothing, not a hint of recognition or foreknowledge concerning what he was about to say. If she did know who he was, she was a world-class actress.

"My wife died two years ago."

Those exotic eyes widened and her mouth dropped. "I'm…I'm sorry. I didn't know. Melissa didn't tell me that. She didn't tell me anything about you but your name."

"Usually that's enough," he said ruefully.

"But then…you don't think I'm going to give you my baby?"

"Our baby," he growled. "As much mine as yours. Assuming of course that you're actually the mother and it wasn't some other woman who donated genetic material."

"No. It's *my* baby. Biologically. I was artificially inseminated." She lowered her gaze. "This was my third attempt. I didn't get pregnant the first two times."

"And you are certain it was my sample that took?"

"They were all your samples." She pursed her lips. "They made the mistake months ago. They only realized after the last time. The time that was successful."

Silence hung between them, thickening the air. Maximo felt his heart rate quicken, his blood pumping hard through his veins. He looked down at her, at those full pouting lips. In that moment his only thought was what a shame it was that he had not made three traditional conception attempts with this woman. She was incredibly beautiful—an enticing mix of strength and vulnerability that appealed to him in a way he didn't understand. He crushed the surge of almost crippling desire that was washing through him.

"So you're capable of having a baby with a man the usual way, and yet you chose to make one with a turkey-baster?" he said, his voice harsh.

Her lip curled in disgust. "That's horrible."

It was, and he knew it. Yet he felt compelled to lash out at her, at the woman who had walked into his home and tilted his world completely off its axis. He hadn't been entirely happy with how his life was, but he had come to the point where he'd accepted it. Now she was here, offering him things he had long since let go of. Only what she was offering was a mangled, twisted version of the dream he and his wife had shared.

"You're a lesbian?" he asked. If she was, it was a loss to his gender. A waste of a very beautiful woman, in his opinion.

Color flared in her cheeks. "No. I'm not a lesbian."

"Then why not wait and have a baby with a husband?"

"Because I don't want a husband."

He took in her business attire for the first time. The extreme beauty of her face had held his attention before, preventing him from examining the rest of her appearance too closely, and he hadn't noticed the neatly tailored charcoal pantsuit and starched white shirt. She was obviously a career woman. Probably intent on having day-care workers raise their child while she set about climbing the corporate ladder. Why have a baby, then? An accessory no doubt, the ultimate symbol of all she had achieved without the help of a man. Distaste coiled in his stomach, mingling with the desire that lingered there.

"Don't imagine for one moment that you will be

raising this child without me. We'll have paternity testing done and if it is in fact my baby, you may yet find yourself with a husband, regardless of your original plans."

He didn't want to get married again. He hadn't even been inclined to get involved in a casual relationship since Selena's death, but that didn't change the facts of the situation. If this was his child, there was no way he would be an absentee father. He wanted his son or daughter in Turan with him, not half a world away in the United States.

The thought of having his child looked upon as a royal bastard, illegitimate and unable to claim the inheritance that should belong to him or her by right, was not something that settled well with him. And there was only one way to remedy that.

The look of absolute shock on her face might have been comical if there were anything even remotely funny about the situation. "Did you just propose to me?"

"Not exactly."

"I don't know you. You don't know me."

"We're having a baby," he said simply.

"I fail to see what that has to do with marriage," she said, that luscious mouth pursed into a tight pout.

"It's a common reason for people to marry," he said drily. "Arguably the most common."

"I fully intended on being a single parent. I wasn't waiting around for a white knight to sweep me off of my feet and offer matrimony. This wasn't plan B while I waited around for Mr. Right. The baby was my only plan."

"And I'm sure the League of Women applauds your progressive viewpoint, Ms. Whitman, but you are no longer the only person involved here. I am, as well. In fact, you *chose* to involve me."

"Only because I need to know if you're a carrier for CF."

"Couldn't you have had the baby tested?"

"I want to know before the baby is born if there's a chance he or she might have the disease. It's something that would require a lot of emotional preparation. There's testing that can be done *in utero*, but they typically don't perform the test unless both parents are found to be carriers. I could have waited and said I didn't know the father and gotten prenatal testing done but there's a slight miscarriage risk and I just couldn't take the chance, not when I could just come and talk to you. "

"Or perhaps all of your feminist posturing is simply that. Posturing. You said you have a friend at the clinic, and I'm a powerful, wealthy man. It is not outside the realm of belief that you did not receive my sample by accident. How is it that my sample has been sitting there for two years and it suddenly got mixed up with the donor sperm?"

Maximo had seen people go to extreme lengths to get a hand on his money, to use his influence. Had this woman cooked up a scheme in order to net herself money and power? People had done worse for far less than he had to offer, for less than the mother of his child would stand to gain.

"I don't know why the mistake happened, I only know that it did," she said, her pretty white teeth gritted. "But don't flatter yourself by thinking I would go to such trouble to tie myself to you just to get money. In fact, don't flatter yourself by assuming I have any idea who you are."

He barked out a laugh. "It's hardly flattery to assume that a woman who is presumably well-informed and well educated would know who I was. Unless of course you're neither of those things."

Her eyes shimmered with golden fire, her finely arched brows lowered and drawn together. "Now you're measuring my intellect by whether or not I'm aware of who you are? That's quite an ego you have there, Mr. Rossi."

"I'd hate to confirm your take on my ego, Ms. Whitman, but my official title is Prince Maximo Rossi, and I'm next in line for the throne of Turan. If the child you're carrying is mine, then he or she is my heir, the future ruler of my country."

# CHAPTER TWO

SUDDENLY it was horrifyingly clear why he'd looked familiar when she'd first seen him. He wasn't just Mr. Max Rossi. She *had* seen him before. On the news, in the tabloids. He and his wife had been media favorites. They were royal and beautiful, and, by all accounts, extremely happy. Then, two years ago, he'd been in the news for his personal tragedy. The loss of his wife.

She was thankful she was sitting or she would have collapsed.

His dark brows snapped together and she registered concern in his eyes before her vision blurred slightly.

"Are you all right?" He knelt down in front of her and put a hand on her forehead. His skin felt hot and his touch left a tingling sensation behind when he swept his hand down to her hair and moved it aside, exposing her neck to the cool air. She hadn't realized she'd been sweating until that moment.

"Yes," she said. Then, "No."

"Put your head down," he said.

She was far too sick to do anything but comply. He gently tilted her head down, his hand moving slowly up and down the curve of her neck, the action soothing, his touch shockingly gentle despite the strength of his hand. It had been a very long time since anyone had touched her. There had been handshakes, casual contact during conversations at work, but she couldn't remember the last time someone had put their hand on her with the intention to comfort. She hadn't realized how amazing it could feel.

But Maximo's touch was causing little rivulets of sweet sensation to wind through her, the slight rasp of his firm fingers against her skin a source of pleasure rather than the kind of anxiety she might expect. It was amazing how a man's hands could be so gentle, yet so firm and masculine. She looked down at his other hand, which he'd settled on her thigh. It was so different from hers; his fingers long and blunt with clean, square nails, his palms wide and strong.

She could feel the warmth from his hand seeping through her wool trousers and she was shocked at how comforting it felt. And something beyond comforting. Something that made her breasts feel heavy and the air seem thick. She'd thought she just wasn't the kind of person who responded to physical touch. She had never really been tactile or sexual, and that hadn't ever bothered her. In fact, it had been something of a relief. She had never wanted to have a relationship, had never wanted to open herself up to someone like that, to grow to depend on them. As a result she'd gone out of her way to avoid serious romantic entanglements.

Her reaction to Maximo was due to pregnancy hormones. It had to be. There was no other explanation for why a part of her left ignored for so long should suddenly come roaring to life.

"I'm fine," she said, her voice sounding strangled. She covered his hand with hers to move it away and the contact sent a shiver of something purely sexual through her. She jerked her hand back and stood up, ignoring the wobble in her vision. "Thank you."

"Are you sure you're healthy enough to sustain a pregnancy?" he asked, his voice full of concern, though for her or the baby she wasn't sure.

"I'm fine. It just isn't every day a girl finds out she's pregnant with the heir to the Turani throne."

Maximo knew there was no way Alison could have faked the way the color had suddenly drained from her face, no matter how accomplished an actress she was. And now, her golden eyes looked haunted, those pretty hands unsteady. After seeing the expression of pure shock on her face he couldn't really believe that she'd orchestrated anything. She certainly didn't look like a woman who was watching a carefully plotted scheme come to fruition. She looked like a hunted doe, all wide-eyed and terrified.

"It isn't every day a man finds out he's received a second chance to have a child," he said.

"You want the baby," she said, her voice hollow.

"Of course I want the baby. How could I not want my own child, my own flesh and blood?"

"If this is about producing an heir can't you find some other woman to…"

"Enough!" He cut her off, rage heating his blood. "Is that what you think? That it would be so simple for me to forget that I had a child in the world? That I could simply abandon him because he was not planned? Could *you* walk away so easily?"

"Of course I couldn't walk away!"

"Then why do you expect me to do it? If it is so simple, you have this baby and give him to me. Then have another one with a different man's *contribution*."

"You know I could never do that. I could never leave my baby!"

"Then do not expect that I could."

"This is… This is all going wrong," she moaned, sinking into the chair by his desk again and covering her face with her hands.

He swallowed. "Things in life don't always go as we plan. Things change. People die. Accidents happen. All that can be done then is the best thing possible with what remains."

She looked up at him, her eyes glittering with frustrated tears. "I don't want to share my baby with a stranger. I don't want to share my baby with anyone. If that makes me selfish then I'm sorry."

"And I'm afraid I can't let you walk away with my child."

"I didn't say I was going to walk away with your child. I understand that this is…difficult for you, too. But you weren't planning on having a baby. I was, and…"

"I planned on having children for years. It was denied me, first through infertility and then through the loss of my wife. And now that I have the chance again, you will not stand in my way."

He couldn't let her out of his sight, of that he was certain. And his course of action after that was still undecided. Marriage still seemed like the most viable of his options, the only way to prevent his son or daughter from suffering the stigma of illegitimacy. And yet the very idea of marriage was enough to make him feel as if his lungs were closing in. But in the meantime, this woman wasn't going to get any chances to escape from him.

"I have to fly back to Turan to see my personal physician. I'm not undergoing any medical testing in the U.S."

"You and your wife obviously did your fertility treatments here."

Yes, they had. Selena had been raised on the West Coast of the United States and they'd always kept a residence in Washington for vacations. It was the place they retreated to when they needed a break from the stresses of life under the microscope in Turan. That was why they had chosen the clinic in Washington to pursue their dream of starting a family. It was relaxing here…a place they had both felt at ease.

"Yes," he said drily, "but my confidence in the competence of your medical system has declined greatly in the past forty minutes, for obvious reasons. My doctor in Turan will be fast and discreet."

She nodded slowly, obviously not seeing any point in arguing with him. "When do you think you'll be able to have the test done?"

"As soon as I arrive. The health of my child is important to me, too."

She suddenly looked so desolate, so achingly sad, that it made him want to take her into his arms and just hold her, gather her fragile frame against him and support her, shelter her. The sudden, fierce need to comfort her shocked him. Was it because she was pregnant with his child? That had to be it. There was no other explanation for such a burning hunger to keep this woman safe from everything that might harm her. His child's life was tied to hers and that called to him as a man—as a protector—on the most primal of levels.

Alison herself called to him on an even more basic level. Was it some kind of latent male instinct to claim what now seemed to be his? The ache to take her in his arms, crush those soft breasts against his chest, kiss her until her lips were swollen, to thrust into her body and join them in the most intimate way possible, was almost strong enough to overtake his carefully cultivated self-control.

"I'm thinking of taking legal action against the clinic," she said softly. "I'm a lawyer and I'm certain we would have a case."

"I'm certain we would, too, despite the fact that I don't have a law degree," he said wryly. "That would mean a lot of press."

The media circus would be out of control. Sensational headlines for a world that loved nothing more than scandal. And his wife's fertility issues, his marriage, all of it would be thrust into the spotlight. It was the last thing he wanted, both for Selena's sake and his own. There was no point in tearing down her memory—not now that she was gone. Some things were best left buried, and the final months of his marriage were among them.

"You do tend to attract a lot of media attention, don't you?"

"I didn't think you listened to entertainment news."

"I don't. But I do stand in line at the grocery store on the odd occasion, which means I've seen the headlines. I just didn't pay close enough attention to recognize you on sight."

"Or by name."

She shrugged. "I only have so much room in my head for trivia. Then I start losing important information."

A reluctant laugh escaped his lips. He liked that she was able to take shots at him, even in the circumstances. It was rare that anyone stood up to him. Even Selena hadn't done that. She had simply retreated from him.

Maybe if she had been willing to come at him with her anger rather than keeping it all inside…

It was much too late for what-ifs. He pushed thoughts of Selena aside, choosing instead to focus on the problem at hand.

"I would like you to go to Turan with me."

Her thickly lashed eyes widened. "No. I can't. I'm busy here. I have a heavy caseload that demands a lot of my attention. Each one of my clients is extremely important and I can't put anyone off."

"Is there no one else at your office that can take care of that for you? You are pregnant, after all."

"There's no 'pregnant, after all.' I have responsibilities. Responsibilities that aren't going to take a holiday just because *you* want me to."

"I see. So your career is so important to you that you cannot manage to take time off to be there in person for the testing? For something that is so important to our child?"

She stiffened, her cheeks suddenly flooded with color, her pert chin thrust out at a stubborn angle. "That isn't fair. It's emotional blackmail."

"And if that doesn't work I'll resort to some other form of blackmail. I'm not picky."

Her lips were pursed again and he wanted to see her relax her mouth, wanted to enjoy the fullness, the temptation that she presented. It had been so long since a woman had tempted him he was enjoying the feeling. He extended his hand and rested his thumb on her lower lip. Her mouth parted in shock and heat shot from his hand to his groin when the action caused his thumb to dip between her lips and touch the wet tip of her tongue lightly.

Desire twisted his stomach. He wanted her with an

intensity that shocked him. And he wasn't certain the pregnancy had anything to do with that. He wanted her as a man wanted a woman. It was as simple as that.

Suddenly his left ring finger felt bare. It was a strange thing to be conscious of since he'd taken his wedding band off after Selena's funeral. He hadn't wanted to carry the reminder of his marriage with him.

"We have to work something out," he said softly. "For the baby's sake. That means compromise, not blackmail."

She turned her head and broke their contact. "Why do I get the feeling the commoner will be doing all of the compromising?"

His lips turned up. "Now, *cara*, you misjudge me. I'm a very reasonable man."

"I'll have to conduct an interview of the people you've had thrown in the royal dungeon once we get to Turan," she said, a slight bite still evident in her resigned tone.

"They aren't allowed to speak, actually, so your interviews will be short."

He could see a reluctant smile pull at the corners of her mouth. It made something that felt a lot like pride swell in his chest.

"I'll have to call the office to try to arrange for the time off." She took a shaky breath and pushed that lovely strawberry hair off her shoulders. "When do we leave?"

Alison regretted her decision to go with his royal highness almost the moment she agreed to it, but no matter how much she turned it over in her mind, no matter how much she wanted to run from it, she knew she couldn't.

Standing in the first-class lounge and waiting for his

majesty to arrive she tried to calm her nerves, and her morning sickness, by gnawing on a saltine and pacing the length of the room. There was plenty of plush, very comfy looking seating, but she was much too nervous, too edgy, to think about sitting down.

How had everything become so complicated? For the past three years she'd done nothing but plan for this. Everything had been geared toward this, toward the pregnancy. She'd saved her paychecks obsessively, driven a junky car, lived in the smallest, cheapest apartment she could find, in the hopes that when she had her child she could buy a house and stay home with him or her for the first few years. She'd quit her high-stress job at a prestigious law firm in order to better prepare her body for pregnancy. She'd even started a college fund for the baby, for heaven's sake!

And one phone call had annihilated all of it. When Melissa had dropped the bomb about her receiving the wrong sperm from a donor with missing medical records, everything had shattered into a million pieces.

She had been so determined to be smart, to ensure that the father of her child wouldn't put the baby's health at risk. She hadn't wanted to give up her anonymity, hadn't wanted to involve the father in any way, and she certainly hadn't wanted the father to be a man who would claim the baby for himself. It was the worst-case scenario as far as she was concerned.

Maximo had been nice enough to her yesterday, but she sensed ruthlessness in him simmering just beneath that aura of power and sophistication. Even when he was being nice his every command was just that: a command. He was a man who did not ask permission.

He was being civil to her now, working with her, and yet she knew he wouldn't hesitate to play on every advantage he had if it came to it. But she would, too. He may hold more cards by virtue of his wealth and position, but she wasn't a doormat. Far from it.

For now, though, civility seemed to be the order of the day, and she was willing to try to work something out with him, even if it was about the last thing she wanted to do. He had a right to his baby, whether or not she liked the idea of sharing custody. He was as much a victim in the circumstances as she was. He was a widower, a man who had already endured loss and heartbreak. As much as she wished she could go back and change her mind about telling him, she wouldn't be a part of hurting him again.

Alison looked out of the heavily tinted windows that gave the lounge a view of the terminal below. She watched as the automatic doors opened and Maximo strode in, security detail and photographers on his tail. Even with the massive entourage of people, every eye was drawn straight to him. He was as big and fit as any of the men on his security team, his chest broad and muscular, the outline of his pecs visible through the casual white button-down shirt he wore. The sleeves were scrunched up past his elbows, revealing muscular forearms and deliciously tanned skin.

He disappeared from view and a few moments later the door to the lounge opened and he strode in, minus the photographers and security detail.

She couldn't stop herself from taking a visual tour of his well-built body. His slacks hugged his thighs just enough so she could tell they were as solid as the rest of him. And, heaven help her, she was powerless to resist the temptation to sneak a peek at the slight bulge showing at the apex of those thighs.

She lowered her eyes, embarrassed by her uncharacteristic behavior. She honestly couldn't remember ever looking at a man there before. Not on purpose, anyway. She tried to tell herself it was nerves making her heart pound and her pulse flutter. She couldn't quite convince herself.

Maximo approached her and took his sunglasses off, tucking them in the neck of his shirt. Again, totally without permission, her eyes followed the motion and she was transfixed by the slight dusting of dark hair she could see on the tanned slice of chest that was revealed by the open collar of his shirt.

"Glad to see you made it," he said. He seemed totally unruffled by the fact that he'd just had a team of photographers taking his picture. He was maddeningly self-assured. If she'd had camera lenses stuck in her face she would have been worried that she might have had a poppy seed in her teeth from the muffin she'd eaten earlier.

"I said I would be here," she returned frostily. "I keep my word."

"I'm relieved to hear that. You're feeling all right?" He took her arm, the gesture totally sexless, more proprietary than anything else, and yet it made her heart jump into her throat. He was so much bigger than she was, so much stronger. Something about that masculine strength was so very appealing. It was easy to want to sink against him, to let him shoulder some of the stress, to bear some of her weight.

And the moment she did that she could almost guarantee he would abandon her, leaving her half crippled and unable to support herself any longer.

She ignored the little flutters in her stomach and tried to focus on the nausea. Anything was preferable to this strange sort of attraction that seemed to be taking over the portion of her brain that housed her common sense.

"Actually I feel horrible, but thank you for asking."

A slight grin tilted his lips. "You can bypass airport security," he said. "My plane is waiting on the tarmac. One of my security agents will escort you out and I will join you in a few moments. We aren't looking to create a photo-op."

She shook her head. The image of herself, pale as a corpse, plastered over a supermarket tabloid was enough to make her shudder.

One of the bodyguards came in and Maximo gestured for her to follow him out. She bowed her head as she crossed the wet tarmac and headed toward the private plane. She thought she might have seen the flash of a camera from the corner of her eye, but she kept her head down, determined not to seem interesting in any way.

She followed the guard up the boarding platform and into the lavishly furnished private jet. It was massive, its plush carpet and luxurious furnishings making it look like a trendy urban penthouse rather than a mode of transportation. But she'd been to Maximo's house and she'd seen the kind of lifestyle he was accustomed to. She really shouldn't be surprised that he didn't do anything by halves. He was the prince of one of the world's most celebrated island destinations, a country that rivaled Monte Carlo for high-class luxury and enter-tainment. Maximo was simply adhering to his national standard.

The bodyguard left without so much as a nod to her and she stood awkwardly just inside the door, not really feeling as if it was okay to sit down and make herself comfortable.

Ten minutes later Maximo boarded, his expression

grim. "There was one photographer hanging out on the tarmac. But since we didn't board together it's likely you might be mistaken for a member of my staff."

She nodded, not quite able to fathom how dodging the press had suddenly become a part of her life. "Are we the only ones flying on the plane today?" she asked, looking around the space.

"Well, you and me and the pilot. And the copilot. And the flight crew."

"That's awfully wasteful, don't you think?"

His dark eyebrows winged upward and she experienced a momentary rush of satisfaction over having taken him off guard. *"Scusami?"*

"Conducting an overseas flight for two people, who could easily have flown commercial, and employing an entire staff to serve them. Not to mention the greenhouse gas emissions."

He offered her a lazy grin that showed off straight, white teeth. It transformed his face, softening the hard angles and making him seem almost approachable. Almost. "When the U.S. President ditches Air Force One, I'll rethink my mode of transport. Until then, I think it's acceptable for world leaders to fly in private aircrafts."

"Well, I imagine it's hard to get through the security lines at the airport with all that gold jingling in your pocket."

"Are you a snob, Alison?" he asked, amusement lacing his voice.

"Am I a snob?"

"An inverse one."

"Not at all. I was simply making a statement." To keep him at arm's length and annoyed with her if she could help it. There was something about Maximo, something that made her stomach tighten and her hands get damp. It wasn't fear, but it was terrifying.

She had never wanted a relationship, had never wanted to depend on someone, to love someone, open herself up to them only to have them abandon her. She had been through it too many times in her life to willingly put herself through it ever again. First with the loss of her beautiful sister. She knew she couldn't blame Kimberly for dying, but the grief had been stark and painful; the loss felt like a betrayal, in a way. And then her father had gone, abandoning his grieving wife and daughter. As for Alison's mother, she might not have left physically, but the person she'd been before Kimberly's death, before her husband had walked out, had disappeared completely.

Through all of that she'd learned how to be completely self-sufficient. And she had never wanted to take the chance on going back to a place where she might need someone else, where she might be dependent in any way.

But she did want to be a mother. And she'd set out to make that happen on her own. Now somehow Maximo had been thrown into her perfectly ordered plans. Everything had been so carefully laid out. It hadn't seemed as if there was a possibility anything could go wrong. And now those idyllic visions she'd had for her future were slipping through her fingers.

Her baby had a father, not just some anonymous donor of genetic material. Her baby's father was a prince. A prince whose arrogance couldn't be rivaled, and whose dark good looks affected her in ways she didn't want to analyze. So much for the best-laid plans.

"You seem to have a statement for everything," he

said, settling into the plush love seat that was positioned in the middle of the cabin.

Alison took her seat on the opposite side of the cabin, settling primly on the edge of a cream lounge chair. "I'm a lawyer. Making statements is an important part of my job."

Max couldn't help but laugh at her acerbic wit. She wasn't like the women he was used to. She didn't cling or simper or defer to him in any way. Some men might be bothered by a woman like her, threatened by her strength and intelligence. He enjoyed the challenge. And it helped that he was certain he held the upper hand in the situation. Now that he had coaxed her into coming to Turan with him the power balance would be shifted completely in his favor.

It wasn't his plan to force Alison's hand in any way; on the contrary he planned to make her an offer that was too good to pass up, once he figured out exactly what he wanted to do. He could tell that Alison would defend their child to the death if she had to, could see that she would lay everything aside for the sake of her baby. But he would do the same. There was no way he was taking the chance that she might disappear with their baby.

It was a strange thing to him that a woman would be so resistant to the idea of having his baby. He wasn't a conceited man, but he was pragmatic in his view on things. First and foremost, he was royal and extremely wealthy. He was to be the next king of his country and along with that would receive an inheritance worth billions, coupled with the personal fortune he'd amassed with his hugely successful corporation. His chain of luxury hotels and casinos were popular with the rich and famous, both on the island of Turan, and in almost every other major tourist spot in the world.

In the eyes of most women he would be the golden chalice. A ticket to status and riches beyond most people's imaginations. And yet Ms. Alison Whitman had acted as though carrying his baby was equivalent to being sentenced to the royal dungeon—which they did *not* have at the Turani palace, regardless of what she thought.

"And your job is very important to you?" he asked, still unable to understand where a child was supposed to fit into this cool businesswoman's schedule.

"Yes. My job is important. I'm a court-appointed advocate for children. My law firm does the work pro bono with funding from the government. The pay isn't what it could be, but I put in some time at a more high-profile law firm and quickly found that handling the divorces of the rich and petulant isn't very rewarding."

"You're an advocate for children?" That didn't mesh with the picture he'd been developing of her in his mind. He'd imagined her to be a toothy shark of a lawyer. With her sharp wit and obviously keen intellect, combined with her cool beauty, he had a hard time imagining her as anything else.

"It's what I've been doing for the past year. I wanted to make a difference, and I knew that if I was going to get ready to have a baby I couldn't be pushing myself the way we were expected to at Chapman and Stone. Corporate cutthroat doesn't really suit me anyway."

"Then why did you get into law in the first place?"

"It pays well," she said simply. "I'm good at it... It just doesn't suit me. But I worked in the industry as long as I could stand, and then I moved into an area of law that was a much better fit. Children shouldn't have to stand in court and face those who made victims of them. I speak for them. I won't allow those who defend abusers and pedophiles to revictimize a child so that they can line their pockets with a little more cash." She offered him a rueful smile. "I am a lawyer, but sometimes there isn't anyone I hate on the planet more than another lawyer."

Alison's cheeks were flushed, the passion that she felt for her job, for her calling, evident in the way she spoke of it. The woman who was carrying his baby made her living advocating for children. Could he have selected better? It was a turnaround from how he'd felt about her before. Instead of seeing a hard-as-nails career woman, he now saw a defender, willing to fight for the right thing, a woman who dedicated herself to the service of others. It only cemented in his mind what he'd already been considering.

Marriage was not a part of the plan for his life. He'd been married. He'd loved his wife. But not even love and respect had made them happy in the end. It hadn't erased their problems. He hadn't been able to fix it, and ultimately, his wife had spent that last months of her life in misery. That was something he would bear for the rest of his life.

But Alison was carrying his child and duty demanded that he do the honorable thing and make her his wife. Perhaps there was a different protocol when a woman had conceived through means other than sex, but it felt the same to him.

A heavy ache pulsed in his groin area, reminding him that it wasn't the same at all. And yet he couldn't have felt more responsible if the baby had been conceived in his bed rather than a lab. He felt responsible for Alison in much the same way, as though they had made their baby the good old-fashioned way.

And the fierce attraction he felt for her was an added bonus. He hadn't intended to remain a monk for the rest of his life, but neither had he felt ready to enter the world of casual dating and one-night stands again. He'd been married for seven years and it had been more than nine years since he'd been with any woman other than his wife. It was safe to say his little black book was outdated. And at thirty-six, he felt far too old to reenter that world anyway.

In that respect, a marriage between Alison and him would be beneficial. The ferocity of his attraction to her was shocking, but that could easily be attributed to the long bout of celibacy. Men simply weren't made to deny their sexual needs for that long and it didn't really come as a surprise to him that now his libido had woken from hibernation it was ravenously hungry.

The beautiful temptress sitting so primly across from him with her milk-pale skin and flawless figure was what he craved. She was different than his wife. Selena had been tall, her curves slight, but the top of Alison's head would rest comfortably beneath his chin. And her curves—they were enough for any man. Her breasts were lush enough to fill his hands to overflowing. Lust tightened his gut and he shifted to relieve the pressure on his growing arousal, and to hide the evidence of his arousal from Alison. He didn't relish the idea of being caught like an adolescent boy who had no control over his body.

"So you like children?" he asked.

She nodded, a shimmering wave of strawberry hair sliding over her shoulder. "I've always wanted to be a mother."

"Not a wife?"

She shrugged, and he couldn't help but notice the gentle rise and fall of her breasts. "Relationships are complicated."

"So is parenthood."

"Yes, but it's different. A child depends on you. They come into the world loving you and it's up to you to honor that, to care for them and love them back. With relationships, with a marriage, you're dependent on someone else."

"And you find that objectionable?"

"It requires a measure of trust in human nature that I just don't have."

He couldn't deny the truth of her words. Selena had depended on him, and in his estimation he had failed her.

"So you elected to become a single mother rather than deal with a relationship?"

She frowned, her full lips turning down into a very tempting pout. "I hadn't thought of it that way. My goal wasn't to become a single mother. It was to be a mother. I wasn't giving too much thought to the exclusion of a relationship. I was just pursuing what I wanted."

"And this complicates things."

"Very much."

"Is it so bad for our child to have both parents?"

She turned her face away from him and fixed her gaze on the view outside the window. "I don't know, Maximo. I don't think I can deal with everything at once. Can't we just get through the testing and talk about the rest later?"

He inclined his head. "If you like. But we still have to discuss our options at some point."

"I know."

"It isn't what you had planned, I understand that. None of this is what I had planned, either."

Alison knew he wasn't just referring to her pregnancy, but to the death of his wife. Finding a woman he had loved enough to marry, and then losing her—she couldn't even imagine the void that must be left in Maximo's life.

She didn't really want to feel anything for Maximo. Already her awareness of him was off the charts, and it scared her. Adding any kind of emotion to that was asking for trouble.

Romantic love had never really appealed to her, and neither had any kind of intimate relationship. She'd seen the aftereffects of romantic love turned sour in her childhood home, watched her parents fall apart and self-destruct. Her mother had simply folded in on herself, leaving Alison to fend for herself.

When her father had left they'd lost their financial stability. People her mother had considered friends had all but abandoned her. Alison never wanted to find herself in that position, never wanted to place so much of her life in someone else's hands that losing them could undo everything. Those experiences had taught her that she had to make her own way, find her own security, her own happiness.

Every inch of her life had been in her complete control since her disastrous childhood. She could control how good her grades were, and in high school she'd been obsessive about keeping her 4.0 so that she could get scholarships. In college she'd been single-minded in the pursuit of her degree, so that she could get a job that would allow her to remain independent. And every step in her life since then had been carefully planned and orchestrated, down to when and how she would become a mother.

All of that seemed laughable now that she was on a plane, headed to a foreign country with a shockingly handsome prince who also happened to be the unintended father of her baby.

# CHAPTER THREE

HER first glimpse of Turan stole her breath. The island was a jewel set in the bright Mediterranean Sea. Gleaming white rock faces beset with stucco houses dotted the pale sanded coastline. The beach faded into lush greenery, and set into the tallest visible mountainside was a stone castle with masculine angles that gleamed gold in the late-afternoon light.

"It's lovely." Lovely, and yet untamed. Sort of like its master. For all of Maximo's urbane sophistication, there was something about him that was raw and almost primitive. It appealed to her on a basic level she'd hardly been aware of before she'd seen him descending the stairs of his elegant mansion.

The entire flight had been thick with tension, at least on her end. Maximo seemed totally unaffected by her presence. Which was more than she could say for herself. It wasn't as though she didn't *like* men or that she had never felt any kind of sexual desire—of course she had. She simply hadn't acted on it, hadn't wanted to. The very idea typically made her feel as if she was on the edge of a panic attack. Sexual intimacy, opening herself up to someone like that, exposing herself, and possibly even losing some of her carefully guarded control, was usually about the least appealing thing she could think of. And yet something about Maximo ignited a curiosity that was starting to override her normal sense of self-preservation.

"Thank you," he said, his voice full of total sincerity. "It is my belief that Turan is one of the most beautiful places on Earth."

The plane began to descend, taking them low over grassland where cattle grazed free-range. "I wouldn't have thought you could do much cattle farming on an island."

"Not much, but we try to make the most of every natural resource we have. Vineyards and olive groves do well. And our grass-fed beef is almost world renowned. Of course, being an island, seafood is also a large part of our exports. But we don't export as much as we might. My first priority has always been self-sufficiency."

She made a small sound of approval. "What do your duties encompass? Your father is still the official ruler, right?"

He nodded. "I have been put in charge of managing the economy. In the past five years I've managed to increase tourism by fifty percent. With the new luxury casinos and the renovation of some of the historic fishing villages, Turan has become a popular destination for wealthy people looking for a high-profile vacation spot."

She arched an eyebrow. "So you're more of a businessman than a prince."

He gave a low laugh. "Perhaps. Maybe in another life that's what I would have been. But in this one, I'm happy to fulfill my duty. I do have some business interests on the side, but my main responsibility is still to my country."

"And duty is the most important thing?"

"It means a lot to me. I was raised to believe that it was duty before self."

*Duty before self.* And did that mean she had a duty to her child to ensure that he knew his father? If her father had wanted her and her mother had never given him a chance, how would she have felt? Pain twisted her. She would have given anything for a father who wanted her. For the protection and safety it would have represented. Did she have any right to refuse her own child this amazing gift? Especially one she would have given just about everything to have herself? She didn't want to face the fact that having Maximo involved in the raising of their child was the right thing to do. What she wanted was for things to turn out according to her plan. But she knew that wasn't possible now.

The plane touched down on the tarmac and her stomach rose into her throat.

When the small aircraft came to a stop, the stairs let down and Maximo took her arm in a very proprietary manner, his posture stiff. He held her as far from his body as was possible, as though too much contact was beneath his royal self. Which was just fine with her. She was still disturbed by the strange effect he seemed to be having on her equilibrium. It was as though her self-control had gone on vacation and now her body was making up for it by craving a whole host of things that had just never seemed important before.

She would much rather have him be aloof than have him touch her again like he'd done at his house. She could easily remember the slow burn against her lip as he drew his thumb over the sensitive skin. She shivered, trying to shake off the little thrill that assaulted her as the scene replayed in her mind.

A crew of five lined the runway, ready to unload his

royal highness's luggage, and her one little carry-on bag. She'd chosen to pack conservatively since she planned to be back in Seattle in just a few days, but seeing all of his belongings next to her one well-used suitcase made the disparity between their social standing widen before her eyes.

He ushered her into the back of the black limousine that was waiting for them, and she complied, mostly because she was in such awe of the wealth that surrounded her.

Money she was used to. For the early part of her childhood her family had enjoyed quite a bit of luxury, and though there were a few years of poverty after her father left, she remembered what it was like to live in the most coveted home in the cul-de-sac. Even now her income was healthier than most, though she chose to save her money rather than spend it on frivolous possessions.

But this…this was like nothing she had ever encountered.

The sleek limo slid through the wrought-iron gates that served to divide the castle and its inhabitants from the serfs who populated the rest of the island. Massive stone statues of men with swords stood watch by the gates, as if to reinforce the exclusivity of the location.

"No moat?" she asked facetiously as she gazed up at one massive turret that rose from the inner walls.

"No, the crocodiles could never discern between the intruders and the residents, so it made for a lousy security system. Now we just have a silent alarm like everyone else."

His unexpected stab at humor brought a giggle to her lips. "No hot oil, then, either?"

"Only in the kitchen." A small smirk teased the

corner of his mouth and she noticed a small dimple that creased his cheek. Why couldn't he stay austere and distant? It was easier to see him as the opposition when he was being an autocrat, much more difficult to do so when he actually seemed *likable*.

They came to a stop in front of the heavy double doors that were flanked, to her amusement, by formally dressed guards who didn't look so different from the stone soldiers that stood at the gates.

He turned to face her, the full impact of his masculinity leaving her close to breathless. "After the doctor comes to perform the test, we will be having dinner with my parents so that I can introduce you to them."

"Why would you need to introduce me?"

"Apart from the fact that you're a guest, you are also the mother of my child, and their grandchild."

Grandparents. He could even give her son or daughter grandparents, while she…well, her own father was heaven-knew-where and her mother was an extremely bitter woman who drank her issues away and forced everyone around her to listen to her vitriolic diatribes about life and men in general. Alison would never subject her child to that. She didn't even subject *herself* to it unless absolutely necessary.

"This just gets more and more complicated." She put her hand over her face and pressed hard on her eyes, trying to stop tears from overflowing. It was overwhelming in so many ways. Being pregnant, actually knowing she was having a baby, had been change enough, but to add all of this seemed impossible.

"They have every right to their grandchild, as I have every right to my child. Just as much right as you have, Alison. I will not allow you to deny my family this chance."

Anger rolled through her, heating her blood, giving her strength. "By royal decree, is that it? Is this where the dungeon comes into play?"

"What is it with you and dungeons? Do you have some kind of weird fetish?"

"Just concerned I might end up on a twenty-four-hour cable news channel. *American held captive by primitive prince*," she snapped. She pressed cool hands to her cheeks in an effort to release some of the heat that had mounted at his mention of fetishes. As if she would ever, *ever*, let a man tie her up so he could have his way with her.

Oddly, instead of the distaste she expected the thought to evoke, when she placed Maximo in the role of her captor, a sensual thrill tightened her stomach. Completely shocked by the direction of her usually sexless thoughts she turned her burning face away from Maximo and opened her own door, not waiting for any of the overeager staff who had appeared outside the palace, to assist her.

Maximo caught up to her in two easy strides, his long legs eating up the ground much faster than her five foot four inches would allow her to do. "Have I embarrassed you, *tesoro*?"

She ignored him, thrusting her chin up and trying to look unaffected by him, his presence and his innuendos.

He gripped her hand and stopped her from walking, drawing her close to him. Her heart began to pound so hard she was certain he must be able to hear it. Standing this close to him she could feel the heat emanating from his body, smell the heady, masculine scent that was one hundred percent raw, sexual man. One hundred percent Maximo.

Since when had she noticed how a man smelled? Unless she was at the gym and it was in a negative connotation she didn't think she ever had. So why did Maximo's smell appeal to her like this? Why did it make her pulse race and her breasts feel heavy? He wasn't wearing cologne or any other kind of added scent. It was just him.

"I would have thought that a sophisticated career woman like you wouldn't be so easy to embarrass." He brushed his thumb across her burning cheek. She knew she was flushed, could tell by how hot she felt. "But it seems as though I've made you blush, *cara*."

"Stop with the foreign endearments," she said, her voice sounding breathless rather than snappy as she'd intended. "I don't like them."

"Really?" He dipped his head and her stomach dropped. She had thought, for one breathless moment, that he might be leaning in to kiss her. "Most women find them very sexy."

"I'm not most women."

He frowned, his dark gaze searching. "No, you're not."

She didn't know whether or not she should feel complimented by that, but she did. Not that she would let him know it. His words shouldn't have the power to flatter or hurt her in any way. They shouldn't have any effect on her at all. *He* shouldn't have any effect on her. The only thing they had between them was their baby. Their relationship had nothing to do with personal feelings. If not for the mistake at the clinic they never would have met. They ran in totally different social spheres. He never would have given her a second look if it weren't for the baby.

It was important for her to remember that.

"When are you seeing the doctor?" she asked, hoping to distract him, eager to not be the focus of his undivided attention.

"She will come as soon as I call her."

She nodded, not knowing why she'd thought he might need an appointment. Maximo wasn't the sort of man who made appointments. People made them to meet with him, not the other way around.

"When will you call her?" she asked, pretending that all of the edginess she was feeling was over the test, and that none of it was due to Maximo's proximity and the way it made her feel.

"Right away, if you like."

She nodded, her stomach fluttering. "Yes, please. I'd like that."

The doctor came immediately, and Alison followed Maximo and the beautiful young physician into his office. When he'd mentioned having a personal physician she'd imagined an elderly man, not a blonde in her early thirties who was tall and willowy enough to be a model.

It shouldn't really surprise her. Maximo was a handsome man. A *very* handsome man, she amended herself. He was rich. And powerful. Plus, of course, there was that very basic feminine nurturing instinct that likely made women want to heal all of his wounds. He probably attracted women in droves. It was likely he welcomed the female attention. He was in his prime; a powerful, sexually attractive man who probably took pleasure when it was offered.

She felt hot all over again and she tried hard to quell that physical response that had become so darn instant and predictable. Maximo was entitled to do as he liked, with whom he liked, which included the sexy doctor, and that was fine by her. Because she didn't want to engage in those kinds of relationships. She had no desire to sacrifice her independence and self-sufficiency for a few hours of hedonistic enjoyment in a man's bed. None at all.

Besides, she seriously doubted she would actually find it enjoyable. It was fine with her if other women wanted to have affairs just for the sake of them, but she never had, and her aversion to relationships had prevented her from actually finding out about physical relationships in a practical, hands-on kind of way. But she was twenty-eight and she wasn't born yesterday. She had a full intellectual knowledge of sex, even if she didn't have actual firsthand experience, and she couldn't imagine such an intimate activity holding any appeal to her. She avoided intimate relationships altogether. She was hardly going to pursue something so…so…profound with a man when maintaining a healthy distance between herself and others was an important matter of self-preservation, as far as she was concerned.

So why did it make her stomach clench when the beautiful doctor slid her feminine hands over Maximo's arm? The sexy blonde drew his shirtsleeve up and wiped at the inside of his elbow with a small cleansing pad, her movements seeming slower, more sensual than was strictly necessary.

"We just need a little blood," she said, her attention on Maximo, her eyes never once straying to Alison.

Alison had to turn her face away when the doctor drew a phial of dark blood from Maximo's arm. She was never very good with things like that and being pregnant made her feel all the more fragile about it. And the last thing she wanted to do was something as ridiculously weak as passing out in front of him. As much as she imagined he was used to women falling at his feet, she couldn't afford to show that kind of vulnerability.

"All done." The doctor all but purred as she tugged Maximo's shirtsleeve back into place, covering up his sexy, well-muscled arm. "It will take five days for us to run the complete carrier screening. As soon as I know, I'll be in touch. If you need anything before then let me know. I'm always available." The good doctor offered Maximo a sympathetic arm squeeze and Alison couldn't help but think that she knew exactly what the other woman would be *available* for if Maximo needed her.

After the doctor left she and Maximo simply sat, silence stretching between them. Anxiety gnawed at Alison's stomach. A few more days and she would know if there was a chance their child might be affected.

Their child. It seemed so surreal that this stranger was the father of the baby nestled in her womb. At least if the baby had been the product of a one-night stand they would have known each other on a basic level. As it was, they didn't know anything about each other. They didn't even share the physical attraction that most people expecting a baby together would have shared.

*Liar.*

Okay, so she was attracted to him. She'd been attracted to men before. Not like this, but she had been, and she hadn't acted on those feelings. She wouldn't have acted on them with Maximo, either.

"Is there a hotel that you can recommend?" she asked, desperate to break the tension that was thickening the air in the room.

The test was weighing heavily on him, too, she could tell. The corded muscles of his arms obviously tense beneath his well-fitted shirt, his jaw locked tight. He really did care about the baby already. Knowing they shared that made her feel linked to him, even if it was only by one tenuous thread. It was comforting in a way, knowing that someone else cared about the baby. That if something was wrong she wouldn't be alone in hurting for her child. For now at least, Maximo didn't feel as much like an adversary.

"Why would you need a hotel?" he asked, flexing the arm that the doctor had taken blood from.

"I don't want to sleep in a field somewhere. I'm not big on camping."

"You do have a very smart mouth," he said, his focus dipping to her lips. She darted her tongue out to moisten them, feeling very self-conscious of the action as she did it. But with him looking at her like that all she could think about was her mouth, and that made it feel dry. And tingly. His dark eyes conveyed an interest that made her stomach tighten. He was attracted to her, too. The realization made her feel light-headed. It had been one thing to experience the errant desire on her own, but to know he might feel even a fraction of it for her…

Just as suddenly as the interest had appeared in his eyes, it was gone, his expression flat and unreadable. She must have manufactured the moment. There was no other explanation. She wasn't ugly by any stretch; she knew that. Men asked her on dates often enough. She wasn't a beauty queen, though. Maximo's first wife had even made Supermodel Doctor look average: her features exquisitely stunning, her sleek dark hair always styled so elegantly, her slim figure the perfect showcase for designer clothing.

She could remember his wife's face clearly. She'd graced the covers of fashion magazines and had been a minor celebrity prior to her marriage to Maximo. An opera singer who had performed in the most prestigious venues around the world, she'd been talented, beautiful and cultured.

So, it wasn't that Alison didn't have her own brand of beauty. She just didn't have that universal appeal, that unquestionable, unrivaled loveliness that Selena Rossi had possessed. There was no way Maximo could want her. She was average, and he was just as perfect as his wife had been. A demigod of masculine perfection.

And now she was dramatizing.

She licked her lips again and silently cursed herself.

"You will be staying here at the palace," Maximo said, his tone so confident she knew that it absolutely didn't occur to him that she might refuse. Or, if it did occur to him he was supremely confident that he could change her mind.

"I don't need you to put me up. I'm perfectly capable of getting my own accommodations."

"No doubt," he said, flashing her a wry smile. "I imagine your extensive education has left you more than capable of booking your own room. But you're pregnant with my child and I don't want you staying at some hotel by yourself."

"Seedy hotels in Turan, are there?"

"Not at all," he said, dismissing her statement with a wave of his hand. "But that doesn't mean I will allow you to—"

She cut him off, anger bubbling in her chest and spilling over. "*Allow* me? You have no authority to allow or disallow me to do anything."

"You are pregnant with my baby. I would say that

gives me some rights over where you go and what you do."

Her mouth dropped open and she was certain she was doing a fair impression of a shocked guppy. He honestly believed that he had some kind of dominion over her, over her body, because he happened to be the accidental father of her baby!

The fine, gossamer strand that she had felt connecting them earlier snapped.

"That is the most primitive thing I have ever heard. You don't have any rights over me!"

"I want to keep you safe. You and the baby. What's primitive about that?"

"Other than the fact that it's controlling beyond belief?"

"*Che cavolo!* How is it controlling to want to protect you? You are pregnant with my baby and that makes you my woman." He looked completely exasperated, as though she were slow in comprehending something that should be completely obvious.

"*Your woman?*" She ignored the sensual thrill that shot through her. It wasn't something to be excited about. It was insulting. Ridiculous. "I'm not *anyone's* woman. Even if we had…" She swallowed and tried to fight the involuntary urge to blush as she spoke her next words, "Even if we had made this baby the traditional way I wouldn't be your woman. I am more than capable of running my own life."

"Yes. You certainly are," he said drily. "How is that going, by the way?"

"About as well as your life is going I would imagine."

He ignored her tart statement. "What's the point of fighting me on this, Alison? I want you here for your safety and the safety of the baby. If the press figure out who you are and you stay here without my protection they will hound you constantly. And what would happen if you get chased by the paparazzi? You have no idea how ruthless and single-minded they can be." His dark eyes were bleak, black holes of bottomless, intense emotion that stunned her momentarily. And just like that, all of the depth was gone, his expression composed again.

"Is that a…is it a possibility?"

"You saw the press at the airport in Washington. Here in Turan it can be much worse than that."

"Oh." She hadn't really taken that into consideration. Hadn't believed that she might be a point of interest to the media. She'd seen how they'd gravitated to Maximo at the airport, but he was…well, he was worthy of press. And they had loved his wife, but she had been gorgeous and talented. Alison truly hadn't thought that they might want pictures of her.

"Yes, 'oh.' I will not take that kind of chance with our baby's safety."

"I won't, either," she said softly, hating that he was right.

"I'll show you to your room."

He placed his hand on the small of her back and led her gently from his office out into one of the main corridors of the palace. The casual touch ignited a flash fire of sensation that scorched a path from the point of contact all the way to her toes and up to her fingertips, hitting all kinds of interesting points in between. A pulse beat, hard and heavy at the apex of her thighs, and she squirmed slightly, in an effort to gain some distance and to quell the insistent ache that was making itself known.

She tried to focus on something other than his touch. A touch that meant nothing to him, and shouldn't mean anything to her. She looked around, taking in her surroundings and gritting her teeth against the onslaught of sensation that was rioting through her. The wing of the palace they had entered was his own personal quarters, and rather than resembling the interior of a Gothic castle it had a light, modern aesthetic that was similar in appearance to his home in Washington.

The walls had been textured and were painted a bright white that contrasted with bold pieces of artwork and sleek, dark furniture. Whoever Maximo had hired to decorate had excellent taste. Maybe his wife had done it. The thought made her chest tighten.

He led her to a curved staircase, winding his arm around her waist and placing a hand over her stomach as they walked up to the second floor. She found the proprietary nature of the gesture oddly comforting rather than offensive, and that scared her. When they reached the landing she moved away from him, not wanting to draw any kind of comfort from his touch. That was not a road she was willing to go down.

He pulled her to him again, placing his hand back over her flat stomach, slowly pushing the hem of her shirt up, his dark eyes intent on hers. He stroked his fingers slowly over the bare skin of her belly, as though he had every right to. It wasn't a gesture of ownership, but an acknowledgment of the fact that they shared something infinitely special.

Tears stung her eyes. It was his baby that she carried and she couldn't deny the connection that he felt with their unborn child, or the connection it made her feel with him. His touch felt right, so right that the steadily growing anxiety that had been gnawing at her since her phone call about the lab mix-up was momentarily masked by the comfort the simple contact gave her.

She looked down at the place where his hand rested on her, his golden skin contrasting with her pale flesh. It fascinated her, held her attention, made her stomach tighten with a deep kind of longing that went way past the desire for something simply physical. But that was there, too. Part of her wished that he would continue moving his hand upward, palm her breast, squeeze her aching nipple between his thumb and forefinger.

She looked up, trying to break the spell that he had somehow woven around them. His face was inches from hers and she was awestruck by the perfection of his striking features. Even close up she couldn't find a single flaw with his sensual mouth, his strong nose and jaw, his dark, compelling eyes. She found herself moving closer to him, leaning in, drawn by an instinct she couldn't understand or control.

When his mouth brushed hers she held her lips still for a second. Then he moved, pressed his hand to the small of her back, closed the gap between them and brought her up against his hard body. She parted her lips, allowing the tip of his tongue to delve between them, to lightly tease her. It wasn't a demanding kiss. It was a slow seduction of her body, her mind, her senses. She'd never been kissed like this, with this level of skill and sensuality.

She'd kissed men before. Mostly back in college when she'd bothered with the pretense of casual dating. But never had a kiss made her feel so hollow, so desirous for more, as if she was in need of something only this man possessed.

Always, the kiss itself had been the main event for her. Other kisses had either been nice, or not so nice, but never had they made her want to lean in, to press her body more firmly against a man, to rock her hips against his hard length to bring herself at least some small measure of satisfaction.

His tongue slid over hers and she felt it all the way in the core of her body. Muscles she'd never been aware of before clenched in anticipation of something much more intimate.

When Maximo pulled away she swayed slightly, her brain totally scrambled by the drugging power of his lips covering hers.

"Max," she whispered, touching her lips, feeling for herself that they really were swollen and hot from the press of his mouth against them.

His mouth curved into a slow smile. "Max. I like that."

The fog of desire was starting to clear and awareness was creeping into the fuzzy edges of her mind, shame mingling with her slowly ebbing arousal.

He placed his hand over her stomach again, his expression intense. "This is my baby that you carry, Alison. Our baby. I could not feel it more if you had conceived in my bed." His accent was thicker than she'd ever heard it, his voice a husky rasp that made her nipples tighten and her pulse pound. "The attraction between us is very convenient."

"Convenient?" Her tongue felt thick and clumsy, her mind still clouded by passion.

"Of course. How could it not be convenient for me to feel desire for my future wife?"

# CHAPTER FOUR

"YOUR future wife?" Her head was still fuzzy from the kiss, her limbs heavy with arousal, and she was certain she must have heard him wrong.

"Yes. I have thought it through and it is the only thing to be done." He said it so pragmatically, as though anyone should be able to see his point.

"I'm not going to marry you," she said, trying to match his tone. If he wanted to try to have an insane discussion as calmly as if they were talking about the weather then she was more than up to the challenge. She certainly wasn't going to give him the satisfaction of rattling her self-control more than once in a five-minute time span.

"Alison, I credit you with a very high level of intelligence, and given your career choice it's obvious to me that you're not only very smart, but very compassionate. With those two qualities I can't imagine that you have not arrived at the same conclusion as me."

"I fail to see how intelligence and compassion would lead me to conclude that you and I should get married." But darn if it didn't make her heart thunder harder in her chest. The thought of being married to a man like Maximo made her stomach turn over, and not in an unpleasant way.

"Logic would tell you that we won't be able to share custody as well as we might if you are living in the U.S. and I'm living here. Also, there would be the added stigma of my child being illegitimate. An illegitimate child will not be eligible to assume the throne, neither will they be able to claim the bulk of their inheritance. Compassion would prevent you from allowing that to happen to our son or daughter."

She shook her head. "That's your version of logic, but that can't possibly be the best thing for our child. We don't even know each other. How could it be good for them to grow up in a home where their mother and father are essentially strangers?"

"But we would not be strangers," he said, supremely confident. "We share some pretty combustible passion. I think we would become acquainted very quickly."

"I don't even know you. You expect that I would just sleep with you?"

He shrugged. "It is not unheard of for strangers to sleep together. And anyway, if we were married it would only be natural."

For him it might be natural to just sleep with a woman because he wanted her. For her there was nothing natural about it. Nothing natural at all about the idea of getting naked with him, of letting him touch her everywhere, see her totally uncovered. Her whole body tensed at the thought.

She tightened her lips and forced her expression to remain neutral. "Sorry, I'm not in the market. If you re-member from previous conversations I'm not interested in snagging myself a husband."

"Yes, that was your original plan. But things have changed."

"Nothing has changed. Not really. My goals haven't changed."

His jaw tensed. "But the reality has changed. Believe me, marriage was not on my 'to do' list, either. I've been married. I don't believe I have the ability to fall in love again. No woman will ever replace my wife."

"Don't break your no-marriage vow on my account."

He cupped her chin and tilted her face up. "I wouldn't be breaking it on your account. This is for our child. I thought you would be able to see that, and that it would matter to you."

"Don't for one moment imply that the baby's happiness doesn't matter to me!"

"Then do not act like it. It's selfishness, Alison, pure and simple, for you to refuse to marry me." His dark eyes glittered with dangerous heat and an answering spark ignited in her belly, anger and desire acting as accelerants.

"And it's plain bullheadedness for you to think that you have the only answer!"

"So passionate," he said, his voice low and husky. He slid his hand up so that he could put his palm on her cheek, the slight roughness of his skin creating delicious friction. "It's a shame you choose to express it this way."

"How would you have me express it?" she snapped.

"In my bed," he said, each word succinct.

"That's about as likely as me taking a trip down the aisle," she returned.

A wicked, dangerous, smile curved his lips. "That, *cara*, sounds very much like a challenge, and I'm the wrong man to issue a challenge to."

"Sounds like you're issuing a challenge of your own,

Maximo. And believe me, you might be bullheaded, but I'm not exactly a shrinking violet."

"I believe it. That is why I find you so intriguing. You are a woman who knows her own mind."

"That's right," she bit out, "and my mind says that marrying you would be a very stupid thing to do."

"It is the only logical thing," he said. "I trust you will come to the same conclusion."

He turned and continued walking down the corridor, acting as though the conversation hadn't happened. She followed, if only because she didn't relish getting lost in the labyrinthine hallways of the palace, especially since she had no soda crackers at her disposal and she was beginning to feel nauseous again. If not for that, she might have taken her chances.

Maximo didn't say another word as he walked and she was more than happy to maintain that status quo. Instead of talking, she played the conversation over in her mind. Was he right? Was marriage the only option?

In the U.S. she hadn't considered being a single mother an issue. But this was a different country, and not only that, her baby was royalty.

A wave of sadness washed over her. It wasn't what she wanted for her child. She had dreams of sitting at a small kitchen table, eating family dinners, coloring, finger painting. Never had she imagined pomp and circumstance and palaces. If she were to marry Maximo their child would be next in line to the throne. And if she didn't, he or she would be off the hook. She honestly wasn't certain which scenario was best. She'd had dreams of a normal childhood for her son or daughter, but what would *they* want? Would they hate her for denying them not only an intact family, but a place in history? It was too much to even take in.

The only thing she was remotely certain of was that she wanted the very best for her baby. If only she could figure out what that was.

"This is your room." Maximo opened one of the doors and gestured for her to go inside.

She looked back down the endless hallway and cursed the fact that she hadn't been counting doors on her way down. She was never going to find her way back.

"Don't worry, I'll escort you back later," he said, amusement lacing his voice.

"Businessman, prince and mind reader?" she asked.

"I promise you I can't read minds. Faces are another matter. And you have a very expressive face."

She put a hand to her cheek. She had always prided herself on control, and that included control over what she let others see. She didn't like that he had the ability to read her.

"Don't worry," he said laconically, "it wouldn't be obvious to everyone. But when you are worried you get a little crease between your eyebrows."

She rubbed at the spot absently, trying to smooth it. "Well, who doesn't?"

"You don't like that I can read your emotions?"

"Would you like it if I could read yours?"

He frowned. "I don't consider myself an emotional man."

"You showed plenty of emotion when you found out about the baby," she said softly.

"Yes. Of course I did. The love a parent feels for a child is above everything else. It's as natural as breathing."

"Not to everyone." She thought of her own father,

unable to love anyone anymore after the loss of his youngest daughter.

"It is to me." He shifted, his jaw clenched tight, the tension evident in his entire body. "Selena and I wanted very much to have children."

For the first time Alison wondered what it must be like for him to be having a baby with a woman who wasn't his wife. She'd had plans, dreams that hadn't included him, and it was the same for Maximo. When he'd pictured having children he had imagined sharing it with his wife, the woman that he loved. As far removed from perfect as this was for her, it must be much more so for him. Her heart squeezed. She didn't want to feel sorry for him, didn't want to understand him, didn't want to see, even for a moment, why he might be right to ask her for marriage. But she did. In that moment, she did.

"Why don't you go in and rest for a while. We'll meet my parents for dinner in a couple of hours. Your things should already have been brought in." Maximo seemed to be done discussing the past, and she wasn't going to press him for more.

She stepped into the room and her eyes widened. It was decked out for a princess. From the plush cream carpets to the lavender walls, the rich purple bedding and the swags of candlelight fabric that were draped over the canopy bed frame. This bedroom was a feminine fantasy. And she couldn't help but wonder who the fantasy had been created for. The prince's mistresses? She could hardly imagine a man like him would be without female company for very long.

Completely without permission her mind began to play a slideshow of what that might look like. She could see it clearly. Maximo's hands gripping a woman's rounded hips, his dark hands covering full breasts, kissing the white column of his lover's throat. And when she saw strawberry blond hair fanned out over the pillow she blinked to try to banish the images. A hot tide of embarrassment assaulted her when she realized she'd cast herself in the part of Maximo's lover. It was laughable. Apart from the fact that she had no desire to sleep with him, there was no way he would want to take a twenty-eight-year-old virgin to bed.

She knew that some men got off on inexperience, on being a woman's first lover, but she had a feeling that at her age it ceased to be sexy and started to look a lot more as if there must be something wrong with her.

"This is nice," she managed to squeak out through her suddenly tight throat.

"Glad it meets with your approval. Is there anything you'd like to have brought up to you?"

A sudden roll of nausea assaulted her. "Yes. Saltine crackers. And a ginger ale if there's one handy."

He drew his eyebrows together, his expression full of concern. "You are not feeling well?"

"I'm never feeling well these days."

"This is normal?"

She shrugged. "Morning sickness. Although mine lasts most of the day. But yes, that's normal for some women."

"Rest," he said, his tone commanding. "I will see that you are cared for."

Suddenly she was so tired her only wish was to comply with his command. "Thank you."

He turned and left the room, closing the door behind him, and she stumbled to the bed and climbed on top of it, relishing how she sank into the soft bedding. She didn't bother to take her shoes off or to get under the covers, and in a matter of seconds she was completely dead to the world.

When Maximo returned to Alison's room half an hour later with her requests she was sound asleep, her arm thrown over her face, her hair spread into a golden-red halo. His eyes were immediately drawn to the gentle rise and fall of her generous breasts. She was an amazingly beautiful woman.

Kissing her had been shockingly exciting. He couldn't remember the last time simply kissing a woman had aroused him so much. Maybe when he'd been a teenage virgin, but certainly not any time in the twenty years since then.

He hadn't intended to kiss her. Not yet. Seduction wasn't the way to win Alison over to his way of thinking. She was cerebral; the way to appeal to her would be through logic and reason, not through sensual persuasion. At least that's what he'd thought. She'd been surprisingly passionate in his arms, a little hesitant, but she'd been all the sweeter for it.

The temptation to join her in the bed, to lift the hem of her shirt again, touch her flat stomach and move higher to the lush swell of her breasts, was so powerful his teeth ached. It wasn't only his teeth that were aching, either. He steeled himself against the hot flood of arousal that was coursing through him, fighting to maintain control over his body.

"Alison, *cara*." He reached out and touched her bare arm and desire raced through him like a shot of pure liquor into his system. She was so beautiful. So different from any other woman he'd been with or even wanted to be with.

Always he'd gravitated to tall, slender women.

Models, actresses, women with style and sophistication. Alison was slender, her waist small, but she had a woman's curves; her hips rounded, her breasts enticingly full.

Unlike the extremely fashionable women he'd preferred in the past, Alison seemed to dress simply to stay warm, or to avoid indecent exposure. There was nothing unflattering about her wardrobe, but there was nothing especially flattering about it, either. It was as though she honestly didn't give it a second thought. She had been wearing some makeup the first day he'd met her, but today she'd gone without it entirely. Most women of his acquaintance would have moaned about how pale they looked without it in an effort to get some sort of compliment. Alison didn't seem to care either way.

She shifted beneath his hand, a sweet moan escaping her lips. Her eyes fluttered open and she fixed her sleepy copper gaze on him, her full lips turning up slightly.

"I know you're half asleep," he said softly, "because that's the only way I could have earned a smile from you."

Just like that her brow creased and she frowned. "Oh," she said softly, putting her hand on her stomach.

Anxiety shot through him. "Is everything all right?"

"Everything's fine. Well, my stomach hurts and my mouth is really dry, but everything's fine with the baby."

"That's why I brought your requested items." He gestured to the tray that was sitting next to her.

The crease between her eyebrows deepened and her lips tugged further down at the corners. "You brought me saltines and ginger ale?"

"Not just any ginger ale." He picked the long-stemmed

glass up from the tray. "My personal chef mixed it especially for you. It has fresh ginger and honey, good for your nausea."

She extended a shaky hand and took the glass from him, lifting it to her lips. Her expression turned to one of relief almost immediately. "The ginger is amazing. It solves all my problems. All my physical problems, anyway."

"Still viewing all of this as a problem?"

She took another sip of her drink and shot him a hard look. "Well, yes, morning sickness *is* kind of a problem. Anyway, you can't tell me you're ecstatic about this."

"I'm not sorry about it."

"How is that possible?"

"I want to be a father. I had given up on that ever happening. There is no way I can regret this."

She lowered her head and pressed the glass to her forehead. "I don't know what to do."

"Marry me. It's the best solution. For the baby. For us."

Her head snapped up. "Why is it the best for us?"

"If we were married we would have our child all the time. No missed Christmases, none of this every-other-weekend business. If we had shared custody there is no way you or I could be there for everything."

"That's true," she said softly.

"And I can't imagine that you intend to spend the rest of your life without a man. You're what, twenty-nine?"

Her copper eyes narrowed. "Eight."

"Either way you're far too young to embrace a life of celibacy. Raising a child and having a personal life is not easy. If we were married, that would be taken care of. You and I share a pretty potent attraction, you can't deny that."

"I'm not exactly concerned about the baby's impact on my sex life," she said drily, pulling a cracker off the tray.

"Perhaps not now, but eventually you will be. I can also offer you financial security. You would be free to do what you liked."

"I could stay at home with the baby?"

"If you like. Or you could continue to work and our child would be provided with the best caregiver available."

"I wouldn't keep working," she said.

"I thought your career was important to you."

"It is. But raising my child, being there for everything, that's more important to me."

Maximo only looked at her, his eyebrows raised as if he were waiting for her to continue. Alison wasn't sure how to explain how she felt to him, or if she even wanted to.

She wanted to be the kind of mom who was there when her child got home from school; she wanted to have cookies baked, and to drive them to soccer practice. She wanted to be there, be interested, be involved. She wanted to be everything neither of her parents had bothered to be.

"If that's what you want then I can't imagine you want to spend a good portion of our child's life shuttling him back and forth between households."

She bit her lip so hard she tasted blood. "Well, it isn't as though we're bitter exes. We could share some of the time together. I could stay here sometimes."

"And you think some kind of pieced-together living arrangement would be better than an intact family?"

"What I think is that we have an extremely unconventional situation and you're playing like we can make it into the perfect, model family, when that just isn't realistic."

"I'm trying to do the best thing. You're the one that's too selfish to do the right thing by our son or daughter."

She took another swallow of ginger ale to prevent herself from gagging. She'd been touched when she'd realized that he'd brought her the crackers and soda, but she was much less impressed now that she realized he was just using it as an opportunity to try to goad her into agreeing to marry him.

"I don't understand why you're the one pushing for marriage," she said when she was certain she wasn't going to be sick all over the floral duvet. "Shouldn't it be the other way around?"

A short, derisive laugh escaped his lips. "Perhaps traditionally, but then this is hardly a traditional situation. In this case, I am the one who has the most realistic concept of what it means to be a royal bastard."

"Don't call him that!" she said, putting a hand on her stomach, anger flaring up, hot and fast. "That's a horrible term. No one even uses it in that way anymore!"

"Maybe not in the U.S., or maybe just not in the circles you're in. But I can guarantee you that here, among the ruling class, legitimacy matters a great deal. Not just in terms of what our child can inherit. Do you want our son or daughter to be the dirty secret of the Rossi family? Do you want him or her to be the subject of sordid gossip for his or her entire life? The circumstances of the conception don't matter. What matters is what people will say. They will create the seediest reality they can possibly think of and that will be the new truth. Whether you like the term or not, if you're intent on refusing to marry me, you had better get used to it."

The picture he painted was dark. She could see it clearly. People would stop talking when their child walked into a room, their expression censorious, their rejections subtle but painful.

"You may not want to be married to me, and frankly, I don't want to be married at all," he said. "But you can't deny that it makes sense."

"I just don't like the idea of it."

"Of marriage without love?" Maximo knew that most women would reject the idea, at least outwardly, even if their motive for marriage was truly money or status and not finer feelings at all. "I can assure you that love within a marriage does not guarantee happiness." He didn't like to talk about his marriage to Selena. Inevitably it brought up not only her shortcomings, but his own failures. And neither were things he revisited happily.

"That isn't it." She drew her knees up to her chest, the action, combined with her messy hair spilling over her shoulder and her pale, makeup-free face, made her look young and extremely innocent. "I never planned on marrying at all. So love isn't really an issue. I just don't want to be married."

"Is this some kind of feminist thing?"

She snorted. "Hardly. It's a personal thing. Marriage is a partnership, one that asks a lot of you. I don't have any desire to give that much of myself to another person. Look how often marriages end in divorce. My own parents' divorce was horrible, and during my two years as a divorce attorney I saw so much unhappiness. Those people grew to depend on each other and for one of them, usually the woman, divorce left them crippled. It was like watching someone trying to function after having a limb chopped off."

"I know what it is to lose a spouse," he said grimly, the brackets around his mouth deepening. "You can survive it. And what you're talking about is love gone sour. That isn't what we have. Our reasons for marriage are much stronger than that, and they will be the same in ten years as they are now. Love fades, lust does, too, but our child will always bond us together."

He was right about that. Whether they married or not, Maximo Rossi was a permanent part of her life, because he would be a permanent part of her son's or daughter's life. A key part. One of the most important parts. He was her child's father. Hadn't her own father, or rather his absence, shaped her life in more ways than she could count?

And that was a whole other aspect of the situation she hadn't considered before. It wasn't just the presence of a parent that had an effect on a child, but the absence of one. What would it do to their child to live in a separate country from his or her father? What would it mean for them to be shuttled back and forth?

That was another tragedy she'd witnessed during her time as a divorce lawyer. The way it hurt the children involved. What it did to their self-esteem. Often, the children she helped in her new job, the ones who were on trial for petty crimes, were from broken homes.

She knew she would never let her child fall through the cracks like those children had, but the issue remained the same. If she could offer her son or daughter a greater amount of security, a better chance at success, shouldn't she do it?

But marriage hadn't factored into her life plans. She

didn't want to be a wife. Didn't want to need Maximo. But no matter whether or not *she* needed Maximo her child would.

Logically, if she'd never intended to get married she wasn't sacrificing anything by marrying Maximo. But… she still didn't want a husband-and-wife-type relationship. It was too much. Too intimate. Too revealing. Even without love.

"I don't want to do this," she choked.

"It isn't about what we want, Alison. It's about what's right. What's best for our child. You've already made so many decisions based on that. I know you love the baby already, that you were already prepared to make major changes in your life in order to offer him the very best you could give. Now the best has changed."

It would be so much easier to refuse him if he were simply being an autocratic tyrant, if he were being demanding and arrogant and commanding and all those things she knew he was capable of being. But he wasn't. He was appealing to her need to reason and plan and choose the best, most sensible way to do something. And he was winning.

He was right. The only reasons for her not to marry him were selfish. All of the reasons to marry him benefited their child. If she could see another way she would grab it.

"Okay," she said slowly, feeling the words stick in her throat, "I'll do it. I'll marry you."

# CHAPTER FIVE

A SENSE of triumph, along with a compressing sensation in his throat that felt suspiciously like the tightening of a noose, assaulted Maximo. It was necessary; the only thing that could be done. The only way for him to truly claim his child, make him his heir. And the only way to claim Alison.

A heavy pulse throbbed in his groin at the thought of claiming Alison in the most basic, elemental way. He wanted her with a kind of passionate ferocity that was foreign to him.

He would have wanted her no matter what, would have desired her had he passed her when she was walking down the street. But the intense, bone-deep need to take her, to enter her sweet body and join himself to her...that had to be connected to the pregnancy because it was outside anything in his experience. He'd experienced lust—the basest kind that had nothing to do with emotion—and he'd been in love. This didn't resemble either experience.

He could satisfy his lust for her without marriage, but marriage was necessary for him to have the sort of relationship with his child that he wanted, that he craved. And it was the only way he could give his child everything he or she deserved.

"My acceptance isn't without provisos," she continued, her gorgeous face deathly serious. "I agree that marriage seems to be the best solution, but don't expect that I'm just going to cave into all of your demands."

"Even after knowing you for only a few days, I would never expect that," he said drily.

She swung her legs over the side of the bed, a cracker still in her hand, and stood. She wobbled and he reached out for her, hooking his arm around her waist to steady her. His response was immediate and fierce, his blood rushing south, his body hardening instantly. He could feel her heart pounding hard against his chest. Her copper eyes were wide, her lips parted slightly. How easy it would be to dip his head and taste her again…

She straightened, much too quickly for his taste, and pulled away, adjusting the hem of her casual T-shirt, her mouth now pulled into a tight line.

"Thank you," she said tartly, moving back from him again, creating even more distance between them. "I'm not feeling very well."

"So you said. Is it like this every day?"

"Pretty much. It hit with a vengeance right when I entered my sixth week."

"How far along are you?" He realized then that he'd never asked.

"Seven weeks."

His stomach tightened. She was nearly two months along already. It wouldn't even be nine months until he held his son or daughter in his arms.

She was still slender, her stomach flat. He had to wonder if her breasts had already changed or if this was her normal shape. He could easily imagine her filling out, her belly getting round. Some previously undiscovered, primitive part of him surged with pride at the thought.

Pride…and a hot tide of arousal. He'd never actually thought of pregnant women as sexy before, but he could very easily imagine running his hands over Alison's bare, full stomach, feeling his child move beneath his hands.

"The baby's due in October," she said.

He'd heard of pregnant women glowing, but he'd never seen it before. Until now. Alison's whole face was lit up, a sweet, secret smile curving her lips slightly. The absolute joy he could see shining from her eyes was staggering. And it reminded him again why marrying her, providing his child with both parents, was the absolute best choice. She would be a good mother; he was absolutely certain of that. Were he not, there was no way he would have considered marrying her. If he wasn't sure of that he would have simply sought sole custody of their child, and he would have done it without compunction.

"You are excited about it," he said, tucking a strand of hair behind her ear.

"Of course I am."

Their eyes locked and held, and the tightening in his stomach intensified, radiating outward, desire gnawing at him with an urgency that was impossible to ignore.

"We'll have to have the wedding soon. Before you start to show," he said, his voice harsher than he'd intended.

She chewed her lip, her eyes betraying insecurity, fear, for the first time since he'd met her. Anger he'd seen, sadness, too, but never this bleak hopelessness. It made his chest ache as fiercely as the rest of his body.

"As I said, there are provisos to my agreement."

"You did say. What you didn't say was what those little stipulations were."

"I don't want our child in boarding school or anything like that. I want him or her to have as much of a normal upbringing as possible. No team of nannies, no catering to his every whim. I don't want a spoiled child, either."

"Do I seem like I was a spoiled child?"

"Yes." She replied without missing a beat, and then continued. "I want to continue being active in advocating for children. Maybe organize a charity or something."

"A wonderful idea. We have several organizations in place and having my princess closely involved would probably do wonders for them."

"And I don't… I want my own room."

He inclined his head. "That is a common practice in royal marriages."

"I don't think you understand. I don't want for us to… I don't want to have a sexual relationship with you."

Alison tried to clamp down the wild fluttering in her stomach. She knew Maximo wouldn't be happy. Hadn't he referenced their physical attraction as a reason for marriage? But this was what she needed in order to be able to accept his proposal, such as it was.

His kiss had decimated her control, had made her forget who she was, who *he* was, where she was. Going to bed with him… What would that do to her closely guarded self-control? The thought of surrendering herself like that, of stripping herself bare both physically and emotionally before another human being in that way, terrified her to her bones. Marriage she could deal with, but sexual intimacy was several steps beyond her.

She was attracted to him; unreasonably so. And that only made her more determined to maintain a healthy distance between them. If she didn't want him like this, if being near him didn't make her limbs weak and her pulse pound in her chest, at the apex of her thighs, if she didn't get embarrassingly wet with wanting just from the brush of his mouth over hers, she might be able to simply deal with it. But it was the ease with which he robbed her of her common sense, her ability to think coherently, that had all of her internal alarms going off. He had too much power over her already, and throwing sex in with that big mess of emotions was a recipe for absolute disaster.

"That makes no sense. You can't deny that we are extremely attracted to each other."

"Maybe not. But I don't feel like I can commit to that sort of relationship with you. Things are complicated enough. A marriage in a strictly legal sense I can handle. But I've only known you for twenty-four hours and I can't even begin to consider a sexual relationship with you. And you're a very attractive man. I'm sure there will always be lots of women who want to…"

"If you're concerned about my fidelity, don't be. I was married for seven years and never once did I look at another woman. It was not a hardship for me."

Maybe not, but Maximo had been in love with his wife. They weren't in love. Not that she cared. But if she were to sleep with him, she would need to know that he was being faithful to her. And that was just one more reason not to cross that line with him. Even imagining a hypothetical situation where they were intimately involved made her care about who he slept with. It made her feel things like jealousy and insecurity, and other emotions she had no business feeling. If she actually made love with him it would no doubt be multiplied by a hundred, and that was just one of the many things she was trying to avoid.

"I'm not concerned about that. But if we *were* sleeping together then yes, I would want you to be faithful. You would want the same from me. Emotions would become involved."

"Not for me," he said starkly. She knew he spoke the truth. But he probably had lots of sexual experience. Divorcing love from sex was probably second nature to him. For her…she knew instinctively that sex could have a seriously devastating emotional effect on her. She just wouldn't be able to open herself up like that to someone without becoming involved. It was one of the reasons she'd avoided it for the past twenty-eight years.

The last thing she needed was for him to become a necessity to her, and she knew that if she let herself she could easily melt into Maximo, let his strength hold her up when things were hard. She could grow to depend on him, and she'd spent far too long learning to be independent, to be in control, to take that chance.

"Maybe not. But this is what I want."

"And you wouldn't mind if I were having sex with other women?" he asked, his words obviously chosen to elicit a response from her. One they most certainly got, but she wasn't going to let him know that.

"I wouldn't care either way. If we aren't sleeping together then there isn't a relationship to be faithful to."

"You may feel differently once we speak our vows."

"I can't imagine that I will. What we have in common is the desire to do what's right for our child. Nothing more. We didn't even conceive in the way most couples do."

"But we very easily could have."

It wasn't true—she *knew* it wasn't—and yet it was far too easy to visualize the image, a picture of her meeting Maximo in a bar, a restaurant, on the street. Of them talking, smiling, laughing. Having dinner together. Going home together. Making love.

*No.* It was easy for him to assume that might have happened, because he figured her for a normal woman who dated, had casual relationships, had sex. She didn't do any of those things. And she had never felt lacking in any way because of it. Until now. Now she felt at a disadvantage. How was she supposed to deal with a man like Maximo? A sophisticated, experienced man who probably knew a lot more about women and sex than the average male. And *she* knew far less about men and sex than the average female.

"Those are my terms, Max," she said softly. "I can't marry you if you won't agree to them."

"Then I agree to them. I don't want a martyr in my bed. I've never had to coerce a woman into sex in my life and I don't intend to start doing so with my own wife."

It was the absolute truth. He wasn't about to black-mail or beg to get a woman to have sex with him, not even one he desired as much as he did Alison. He hadn't even begged Selena when she'd moved out of their room. No was no, even from his wife.

He was surprised that Alison was denying them both what they so obviously wanted, but not even a sexless marriage was new to him. He'd been there. He imagined it had been Selena's way of punishing him for not giving her a baby, although the issue had been with her body and not his. It hadn't mattered to him. He had never once seen her as less of a woman. But she had been so frustrated with their timed lovemaking that never, ever produced the result she wanted, that she hadn't even allowed him to touch her in the last six months of their marriage. The last six months of her life.

He knew why Selena had denied him, and he wasn't sure he hadn't deserved it. But he didn't know what Alison's game was. She was twenty-eight, a career woman, not sheltered or shy in any way. And she was very clearly heterosexual and very clearly attracted to him. So it didn't make any sense for her to turn down a physical relationship with him. Especially since she obviously wanted him. Women might be able to fake orgasms, but her response to his kiss was very real. There was no way she could have engineered her body's response to him, and no reason for her to do so.

But if she needed to put up a pretense of morality by insisting she couldn't sleep with a man she didn't know, she was welcome to do it. Although he doubted that she would hold on to that stance. The attraction between them was far too strong for that. It was certainly beyond anything he'd ever known in his experience.

She licked her lips and his body ached with the need to taste her sweet mouth again, to move his tongue over hers. He was instantly hard, his body raging with his need.

If she felt half of what he did, and based on that explosive kiss they'd shared in the corridor he was certain that she did, her play at resistance wasn't going to last for very long. It simply wasn't possible.

"Are you feeling up to dining with my parents?"

She sucked that sweet lower lip into her mouth and chewed on it thoughtfully. When she released it there were little dents left by her teeth, and he wanted to soothe them with his thumb, his tongue.

"I don't suppose it's acceptable to cancel dinner with the king and queen. What would Miss Manners say?"

His lips twitched and she felt an odd sense of gratification over having amused him. "If you're not feeling well we will cancel."

Selena would have canceled. His wife had frequently felt under the weather. She had been very delicate, emotionally and physically, and he had looked on it as his duty to protect her, shield her. It would be his duty to do the same for Alison. She was under his protection now. And he wouldn't fail her.

The look of steely determination that lit Alison's copper gaze surprised him. "I'll be fine. I've been going to work, cooking my own meals, functioning just fine without being coddled. I'm more than able to meet with your parents."

A brief spark of vulnerability shadowed her eyes. "What are they going to think about all of this?"

He shrugged. "I don't know that the nature of our relationship is any of their business."

"You mean you don't want them to know how the baby was conceived."

"They didn't know about Selena's fertility problems."

"I see." She looked at him, her expression searching. "And you don't want them to know."

"It was important to her that no one knew about her infertility. I have honored that." She had seen it as a failure, one she couldn't face sharing with the public, or his parents.

"Then I don't think it's important for them to know how we conceived the baby." Alison didn't really relish having to keep up any kind of facade, but neither did she want to be a part of damaging his late-wife's memory.

It made her heart break a little to know that she was going to have the dream Selena had been denied, having a baby with Maximo. As much as she would have rather been honest about the nature of her relationship, or lack of it, with Max, she felt she owed the other woman some protection.

"I'll leave you to shower and get ready. I'll be back in an hour."

She watched Maximo, her fiancé, turn and leave the room. A feeling of longing, so intense she felt it physically, filled her. Part of her wanted him, impossibly, irresponsibly, almost as much as the sensible part of her craved distance and protection from him. It was like a tug-of-war, each desire pulling at her from opposite sides. And the sensible part of her had to win. It *had* to.

The dining room at the *castillo* was extremely formal. The high ceilings and ornately framed artwork gave the room a museumlike quality. The long banquet-style table could easily have seated thirty or forty people, and added to the wholly impersonal feel of the room. It made stupid, emotional tears prick at her eyes.

A child couldn't sit and color at this table. They certainly couldn't eat milk and cookies and peanut butter and jelly at this table. Finger painting was probably out, too, since it was likely a priceless antique.

Of course, she knew there were other tables in a place this big. Maximo's quarters likely housed its own dining room. But what this room represented was everything she feared. Not for the first time since she'd said yes to Maximo's proposal she wondered if she'd made the right choice. It had seemed like it then. His logic had made so much sense. But now…it seemed impossible standing at the entryway to this formal, forbidding room with two equally formal, forbidding people staring at her and Max, his arm clamped tightly around her waist, looming over her.

"Come in and sit down, son." The king gestured to a place at his right at the head of the table. "We're both very interested in why you've asked to have dinner with us tonight."

The king was obviously a man of advanced years, but there was nothing frail about him. His hair was silver-gray, his skin tanned and healthy-looking, wrinkles almost entirely absent from his face. The queen was beautiful, years younger than her husband, her dark hair drawn back into a tight bun, her face also free of lines. They were both terribly intimidating and neither one of them offered a smile as she and Max moved into the room to sit down at the table.

The only friendly smile on offer came from a young woman who was sitting to the left of Queen Elisabetta. Her full lips stretched into a grin that showed her bright white teeth. With her golden skin, dark hair and shockingly blue eyes, she was one of the most beautiful women Alison had ever seen. A strange feeling settled in the pit of her stomach.

The woman jumped up from her seat when they approached and ran to throw her arms around Maximo. "Max!" she cried. "I'm so happy you've come home early!"

"It's good to see you too, Bella." He dropped a kiss on the younger woman's head. "Alison," he said, tightening his hold on her waist, "this is my younger sister Isabella."

The suspicious knot that had been tightening in her stomach released its hold on her as soon as he announced his relationship to the very beautiful Isabella. She was relieved, she realized, to find out that she was his sister and not...

She cut off that train of thought before it could go any further. It wouldn't have mattered if she were a lover or a former lover. It wasn't her business. And there was no reason for her to care.

"Nice to meet you." Isabella dropped a light kiss on Alison's cheek. "I'm so pleased that Max brought a friend with him." She cast her brother a sly look that seemed to say she had guessed that there was more to the relationship than he'd admitted.

"And these are my parents, King Luciano and Queen Elisabetta." Maximo gestured to his parents who were still sitting, rigid as stone, at the head of the table.

"It's nice to meet you, too," Alison said, grateful at least for Isabella's enthusiastic greeting. "All of you."

Maximo pulled a chair out for her and she sat gingerly, feeling unbearably self-conscious. It was one thing to stand in front of people in a courtroom—that was her domain. She was confident there. She was in control. Here, she was very much the colloquial fish out of water, and she felt as if she was gasping for air.

Isabella offered Maximo an impish smile. "You didn't tell me you had a girlfriend, Max."

Maximo took her hand beneath the table, twining his long fingers with hers and lifting their hands, joined, onto the table. "I was trying to keep it just between Alison and myself until we were certain how serious things were."

Alison nodded—any words she might have spoken jammed in her tightened throat. She hated this. Hated feeling so out of her depth. But, dear heaven, this was as far outside of her experience as anything could have possibly been. She'd never met a man's parents; not in this sense. And these weren't just any parents: they were royalty. And their faces were so stiff she had no doubt they felt she was quite patently beneath them.

"Is it serious?" his mother asked, her eyebrows raised, her lips unsmiling.

"I've asked Alison to marry me," said Maximo simply. It was all the answer anyone needed.

"So soon after Selena's death?" His father's tone and expression were rebuking, and Alison felt a knot of guilt tighten in her stomach.

"It's been two years," Maximo said, his voice firm, "and I have chosen Alison to be my wife."

"It would be best," Elisabetta said slowly, "if you would wait at least a year for the wedding, out of respect to Selena."

"The three-year mourning period is outdated," Maximo said. "I have no intention of waiting another year to make Alison my wife. It is not possible for us to wait so long."

"That's very romantic of you, Max." His younger sister looked positively moonstruck over the perceived romance of the whole situation. If only she knew.

"Romance has very little to do with it," Maximo said, obviously taking no issue with disabusing his sister of her fantasies. "Alison is pregnant. The wedding needs to take place before she starts to show."

Alison wanted to crawl under the table and die of mortification. She was treated to a very shocked look from Isabella and to a couple of very disapproving glares from the king and queen.

"Has there been a paternity test?" The king gave her an assessing glare that made her stomach roll.

"That won't be necessary," Maximo said through

gritted teeth. "I am sure the child is mine, and I never want to hear you suggest otherwise again."

Maximo's rage shocked her. It wasn't as though they were a real couple. He didn't even necessarily like her all that much. It was probably more related to his masculine ego than anything else.

Luciano gave his son a hard glare. "Then there is nothing else to be done," he said. "We will begin planning the wedding immediately."

Queen Elisabetta narrowed her eyes, her mouth pursed. "We know nothing about her, Maximo. Is she suitable? Who are her people?"

Alison shifted in her chair, extremely uncomfortable being discussed as though she wasn't in the room.

Isabella's blue eyes lit with anger. "What does it matter who her people are, Mamma? If Max loves her he should marry her. That's the *only* reason people should *ever* marry."

"This is not about you, Isabella," Luciano said curtly. "But she is right. It is of no consequence who her people are, or where she comes from. She is pregnant with Maximo's heir and that is all that matters."

If King Luciano had stood up from his place at the table and walked over to check her teeth she wouldn't have been surprised. She felt like some sort of royal broodmare. She was acceptable because of the baby she carried. She imagined that if she really had been the woman Maximo loved, if there hadn't been a baby, the king wouldn't be so sanguine about the marriage. He would probably take the stance his wife had. If the damage hadn't already been done she would have been found wanting based solely on her bloodline or her background. She couldn't help but wonder if that were the situation, if they were in love and she were the woman

Maximo had decided he wanted to marry, whose side he would have taken.

She couldn't imagine Maximo being intimidated by anyone. He would never give in to his parents' demands simply because he felt pressured to do so. But he had proven that, above all else, he had the ability to be coldly logical if he needed to be. He didn't want marriage any more than she did, and yet he had immediately accepted that it was the best course of action for the sake of their child. Would he have made the same choice if he felt that marrying the woman he loved conflicted with the best interests for his country?

*Oh, what does it matter?*

She would never know. She didn't need to know, or want to know. She didn't *love* Maximo. She didn't have any feelings for him at all. She *respected* him. Respected his strength, his drive to do the right and moral thing, his love for their unborn child. But that was all.

He moved his thumb over the tender skin of her wrist and a team of butterflies took flight in her stomach, calling her a liar.

So she was attracted to him? It didn't mean anything. He was an attractive man. And then there were the pregnancy hormones. But that was all it was. And thank God for that.

"I'm glad we can agree on this," Maximo said, his tone containing a hint of warning that Alison assumed was meant for his mother.

"We will not have you marry in some civil ceremony," Luciano said, his tone imperious. It was obvious where Maximo had inherited his arrogance from. "You will marry in church, and we will make a formal engagement announcement. We will not treat it like a dirty secret.

You are giving our country an heir and we will celebrate that."

His mother looked as though she had swallowed a lemon. "I suppose a wedding is preferable to the birth of a royal bastard."

Alison sucked in a sharp breath. It was no less offensive hearing it said now than it had been to hear Maximo say it earlier. And she knew now that he'd been telling the absolute truth about how their child would have been viewed had they not married. And it wouldn't have just been the people or the media, but his own family who would have branded their child with that label.

"I won't tolerate hearing our baby talked about like that!" The words tumbled out of her mouth before she could stop them. "I won't allow anyone to hurt my child. Ever."

Maximo cupped her chin and turned her face to him. "No one will hurt our child, *cara*. I will not allow it." He gave his mother a dark look. "This is your grandchild, Mamma. Think about that before you ever say such a thing again."

He stood, and pulled her gently with him. "Alison and I will have dinner in our room." His mother looked offended at that, but she didn't say anything.

Alison elevated her chin, careful not to look defeated in any way. They were just rich, titled snobs. They had no right to judge her. And anyway, she'd dealt with far worse from her own mother. She was hardly going to let venom spewed by a complete stranger make her crumble now.

As soon as they were out in the empty corridor he released his grip on her hand.

"That went well," she said.

"As well as I expected. My mother loved Selena like a daughter. This is difficult for her."

"Then wouldn't it be better if they knew how I got pregnant instead of assuming that…"

"Selena did not wish for my mother to know. She did not want my parents to see her as a failure."

Maximo began to walk back toward his quarters, and she had to take short, quick steps to keep up with his long strides. "That's ridiculous. Not being able to have children doesn't make you a failure."

"It felt that way to my wife." He paused for a moment. "My mother introduced us. It was her opinion that Selena was perfect for me. Her family was wealthy and well-known, she was talented and cultured. In my mother's estimation she would make a wonderful princess. A wonderful mother. When Selena could not fulfill that part of what she considered to be her requirements, she became very depressed."

"But that wasn't the only thing you loved her for," Alison said softly.

Maximo turned to face her, his mouth pressed into a grim line. "No."

"I understand why you don't want it to become public knowledge. I won't tell anyone." It might make things easier in a way, although Alison imagined the queen would dislike her regardless, but she just didn't want to hurt Maximo by dredging up things from the past. And it would hurt him. His expression was always stoic when he talked about Selena, but she had seen glimpses of devastating pain in his dark eyes. And she cared about that. A lot more than she should.

She shouldn't be able to feel his pain in her chest, shouldn't ache for him, want to take his hurts and heal them. She really shouldn't want that at all. But she did.

Her heart hurt for him, felt linked to his. Was that because she was pregnant with his baby? It was a link between them that was impossible to ignore. He was a part of her, in a way.

On the heels of that revelation came a slug of panic. She didn't want to feel so much for him. Didn't want to feel anything for him beyond a circumspect amount of tolerance.

Once they were back in Maximo's quarters he led her into a small dining room that looked as if it belonged in a more casual home. A very, very upscale home, but the room was definitely intended for family use, unlike the massive dining hall in the main portion of the palace.

He sat at the head of the table and it seemed natural for her to sit at the other end. It was easy for her to picture a child sitting between them, chubby fingers gripping a cookie, a big smile on their baby's face. Would their child be fair like her? Or olive-skinned like Maximo? The thought made her stomach tighten painfully, the image of family, their family, so poignant that it touched her more deeply than she'd imagined possible.

This was a new picture, one that was quickly replacing the original images she'd had of life after her baby was born. Now she couldn't help but see Maximo, his presence there both physically and in the features of their child. The ache that settled in her heart was both sweet and scary at the same time. She shouldn't want this. But part of her did. Very, very much.

"Anything special you want to eat?" Maximo asked.

He was so handsome. She couldn't help but notice. With the overhead lighting from the chandelier above the table throwing the planes and angles of his face into sharp relief, making his cheekbones look more prominent, his jaw even more chiseled, he was almost devastatingly handsome. That was a term she'd never understood before this moment. It had never made sense that a person's looks could devastate. But his could. And did. Because looking at him filled her with so much longing, for things she shouldn't want, that it made her heart squeeze tight.

"Honestly, all food sounds basically disgusting to me so it doesn't really matter."

He nodded. "Then I will have the staff bring what they prepared for my parents."

A few minutes later a woman came in pushing a trolley that was laden with silver domed trays. She set two in front of Alison, along with another glass of homemade ginger ale.

Alison didn't even bother to uncover the trays, but went straight for the ginger ale to calm her perpetually unsettled stomach.

"You need to eat," Maximo said. "You are too thin."

She paused midsip. "I'm not too thin! I've been to see a doctor and he said I, and the pregnancy, were perfectly healthy."

"Well, it doesn't seem like you should allow yourself to get any thinner." Maximo rose from his spot at the end of the table and leaned over to uncover her food. There was pasta with marinara sauce on one and what looked like half of a beautifully roasted chicken on the other. But the sight of poultry turned her stomach.

"I might be able to try the pasta," she said, shoving the bird away from her.

Maximo sat in the chair next to her, putting the chicken in front of himself.

"Was your wife on a special diet?" She regretted saying anything the moment the words left her mouth. Usually she was very selective about what she said, but she'd had her fair share of outbursts in the past forty-eight hours. Maximo seemed to have that effect on her.

He shrugged slightly. "Vitamins. Any kind of herbal remedy she could think of. Hormones for the IVF. Plus any food rumored to benefit fertility."

"She really wanted to be a mother," Alison said softly, guilt and anguish almost stealing her breath. Selena had tried so hard to have Maximo's baby, had wanted it so badly, and here Alison was, pregnant with his child. And it had been an accident. It seemed like a cruel joke for fate to play on all of them.

"Yes. She did. We tried IVF three times. We were unsuccessful. She had just taken the final negative test a few hours before her death."

Alison put her hand over his, the gesture intended to comfort. Heat spiraled through her from the point of contact down to her belly. His skin was warm beneath her hand, the hair on his arm crisp and sexy. She'd never imagined that arm hair could be sexy. His was. It reminded her that he was very much a man, and that she was a woman. A woman who was going to marry him in just a few weeks.

She pulled her hand away and set it in her lap, but she could still feel the burn of his skin on her palm. Her heart pounded hard in her chest and an answering pulse pounded in the core of her body, not letting her deny that what she was feeling was definitely arousal. She looked up at Maximo. His eyes were dark, the heat from them searing her, making the flame that had been smoldering in her belly flare up, the fire threatening to consume her at any moment.

She pushed her chair back and stood, desperate to put distance between them. What was it that he did to her that stole all of her ability to think rationally? Being near him, touching him, it took all of that carefully guarded control of hers and stripped it from her, leaving her bare and unprotected.

"I'm tired," she said. "I need to… I'm going to go to bed."

A knowing smile curved his lips. "You are so intent on fighting this thing between us."

"This isn't what I want, Max," she whispered, closing her eyes, trying to block out his handsome face.

"Did someone hurt you?" he asked, his voice suddenly hard.

She shook her head. "Not in the way you mean. But I can't…don't ask me to do this."

"I would never force myself on you."

She knew that. She had no doubts, none at all, that Maximo was a man of his word. A man of honor. But it wasn't the idea of him forcing himself on her that she feared. It was the fact that force wasn't necessary. All he would have to do was touch her, kiss her, and she would forget all of the reasons it was such a bad idea to become physically involved with him.

And she was afraid that, like her mother, if she allowed herself to become dependent she would forget how to take care of herself, and if he left she would just crumble.

She and Maximo were getting married to give their child a family. They were committed to being in each other's lives for at least the next eighteen years. She was already far too dependent on him due to the nature of the situation, and adding feelings, adding sex, had the potential to make it deadly to her.

"I'm tired," she said again, turning to go.

"Get some rest," he said, his voice rough, and she wondered if it was due to arousal; the kind that was making her blood thick and her throat tight. "Tomorrow we will be announcing our engagement to the world."

# Get 2 Books FREE!

## Harlequin® Books,
### publisher of women's fiction,
## presents

# GET 2 BOOKS

We'd like to send you two *Harlequin Presents®* novels absolutely free.
Accepting them puts you under no obligation to purchase any more books

## HOW TO GET YOUR
## 2 FREE BOOKS AND 2 FREE GIFTS

1. Return the reply card today, and we'll send you two *Harlequin Presents* novels, absolutely free! We'll even pay the postage!

2. Accepting free books places you under no obligation to buy anything, ever. Whatever you decide, the free books and gifts are yours to keep, free!

3. We hope that after receiving your free books you'll want to remain a subscriber, but the choice is yours—to continue or cancel, any time at all!

## EXTRA BONUS

**You'll also get two free mystery gifts! (worth about $10)**

# FREE!

Return this card today to get
**2 FREE BOOKS and 2 FREE GIFTS!**

HARLEQUIN®

*Presents*

**YES!** Please send me 2 FREE *Harlequin Presents*®
novels, and 2 free mystery gifts as well. I understand
I am under no obligation to purchase anything, as
explained on the back of this insert.

*About how many NEW paperback fiction books have
you purchased in the past 3 months?*

| ❏ 0-2 | ❏ 3-6 | ❏ 7 or more |
|---|---|---|
| E7RQ | E7SQ | E7S2 |

❏ I prefer the regular-print edition    ❏ I prefer the larger-print edition
106/306 HDL                 176/376 HDL

FIRST NAME          LAST NAME

ADDRESS

APT.#          CITY

STATE/PROV.        ZIP/POSTAL CODE

Visit us at:
www.ReaderService.com

▶ DETACH AND MAIL CARD TODAY! ▶

(H-P-04/11)

If offer card is missing, write to: The Reader Service, P.O. Box 1867, Buffalo, NY 14240-1867 or visit www.ReaderService.com

# BUSINESS REPLY MAIL

FIRST-CLASS MAIL     PERMIT NO. 717     BUFFALO, NY

POSTAGE WILL BE PAID BY ADDRESSEE

**THE READER SERVICE**
**PO BOX 1867**
**BUFFALO NY 14240-9952**

NO POSTAGE
NECESSARY
IF MAILED
IN THE
UNITED STATES

# CHAPTER SIX

ALISON shifted and winced as the boning in the corset top of her gown took another dig at her side. It was hot. Dear heaven was it hot! And humid. Stray wisps of her hair hung down out of her glamorous updo in lank strands. The air seemed thick, and breathing it in only seemed to increase the nausea that was her constant, reviled companion.

The servant that had helped her get dressed had insisted that this was a formal announcement and would require formal dress. So here she was, made-up, sucked in, pushed up and buffed to a highly glossed sheen, waiting behind a heavy red curtain for her time to step out onto the balcony with Maximo so they could make a horribly clichéd announcement to the television cameras and the citizens who had gathered below.

It wasn't just the people of Turan that were watching, but the world. Maximo was charismatic and popular, both in his home country and abroad, and his wedding would be attended by the rich and famous from every corner of the world. No pressure, though. She almost laughed at that thought.

She took a deep breath and tried to ignore the fact that her breasts seemed to be trying to make an escape from the sweetheart neckline of the gown. She imagined it was supposed to be demure, in its jewel-tone sapphire color, with cute ruffled cap sleeves. And it might have been, if she hadn't been quite so generously endowed up top.

She could hear Maximo out on the balcony, on the other side of the curtain, addressing his people, speaking in Italian. If there was a sexier sound in the world she'd never heard it. His voice did things to her, and not only her. He was an amazing public speaker; she could tell from behind the curtain. He had charisma. She couldn't understand a word he was saying but it sounded good.

He was the sort of leader that inspired. The sort of leader his country needed.

She straightened and nearly cursed out loud when the boning dug into her again. She was making the right decision. Maximo was a good man. He would be a wonderful example for their child, and a wonderful father. No matter how overwhelming all of it seemed to her, this was her son's or daughter's legacy. The people waiting down there were her child's people. There was no way she could have denied them this chance.

Luigi, the man who coordinated most big events for the royal family, signaled for her to make her entrance onto the balcony. He swept the curtain aside for her, careful to keep himself out of view, and she took a tentative step out into the blinding Mediterranean sunlight.

The height, the heat and vibrating sea of people below made her head swim. She tried to paste a smile on her face, as she had been instructed to do, and took her place at Maximo's side.

He put his arm around her waist and drew her close. His father, who was standing with the queen, took the center of the balcony and spoke into the microphone. A cheer erupted from the crowd.

Maximo turned to her and brushed her cheek softly with the back of his hand. The light touch sent a shimmer of something wonderful through her. His eyes were intent on her face, his expression serious, but almost caring.

He leaned in and pressed a light kiss to her lips. She hadn't been expecting a gesture of affection like that and it had her heart pounding so hard she was afraid the microphones would pick it up, and everyone would be able to hear for themselves just what Maximo did to her. He held her tightly against his body, his strong arms cradling her. She shifted and her breasts brushed his hard, masculine chest. Electricity zinged through her.

She couldn't stop staring at him, couldn't tear her eyes away from him. Her future husband. He was so handsome dressed in a traditional mandarin-collared suit with a long dark jacket that accentuated his broad chest, slim waist and spare hips. The plain jacket was adorned with medals pinned to the right breast, over his heart. The Latin words written on the pin spoke of duty to God and country.

An intense feeling swelled in her chest. Pride, she realized. She was proud to stand by his side. Proud that he was the father of her baby. And who wouldn't be? He was a *good* man, a man who understood responsibility, a man who valued honor. Maximo wasn't the kind of man who would walk away from his responsibilities. He was the kind of man who would stand and face challenges when they came. When the results of the test came, the test that would tell them if there was a chance their child might be affected by Cystic Fibrosis, Maximo would face it head-on, of that she had no doubt.

He wouldn't run from a painful situation, wouldn't walk away if things were hard.

Maximo leaned in again, his hot breath touching her neck, making goose bumps break out over her skin, despite the heat.

"Wave at your people," he commanded gently. She turned, still in his arms, and put her hand up in a shy wave. She was greeted by another round of enthusiastic cheering. Many of the people waved back or waved flags.

"*Bene,*" he whispered near her ear and nuzzled her gently with his nose.

Lightning flashed through her from that simple brush of skin on skin, igniting a desire that was hot and insistent, and totally outside of her experience. It was all for show. She *knew* that. It didn't mean anything to him. But her body didn't seem to know, much less care. She felt her knees weaken and she slumped against him, against the solid wall of his body. She realized how easy it would be to just melt into him, to lean against him forever.

The strength of those feelings shocked her, made her knees shake. She wasn't supposed to feel like this. She moved then, turning her body away from him, trying to keep her lips glued into a smile. And then she was being ushered back behind the curtain, leaving the king and queen to continue speaking to the crowd.

"You did very well," Maximo said, releasing her from his hold once they were out of view.

"A smile and a wave," she said breathlessly. "Not too impressive."

"When a woman looks like you, that's about all it takes. They loved you."

She laughed shakily. "It's the dress."

"It's a lovely dress." His eyes traveled over her, over each of her curves.

For once, such a close inspection didn't make her think of what might happen if she let a man get too close to her. It lit a fire that smoldered hot in her belly.

It wasn't virginal nerves that made her draw back from the obvious attraction between them. It was a different kind of fear. Fear of the strength of her response to him, of the almost overwhelming need she felt to melt into him, have him assuage the ache he made settle between her thighs. The intense desire to allow him to make her lose control.

"You are truly beautiful." His eyes, those hard, dark, commanding eyes, softened. He cupped her cheek and let his thumb trace her upper lip.

The curtain was swept aside again and the rush of heat that came from outside broke the bubble they'd been cocooned in.

"It is done," Luciano said firmly. "The wedding will take place in eight weeks, after Sunday Mass." He turned to Maximo and said something in his native language.

A dull red stained Maximo's cheekbones and his eyes hardened, a muscle in his jaw jumping with tension. "*Si*. I am certain."

"It's good to be sure." Luciano patted his son on the back before stopping in front of her. "Make him happy."

Luciano and Elisabetta exited the room, leaving Alison and Maximo alone.

"What did he say?" she asked, knowing it hadn't been flattering to her.

"It isn't important."

She let out an inelegant snort. "For something unimportant it certainly made you angry."

"He asked if I was certain it was my child."

That stung a little bit. But then, the king didn't know her. He had to suspect that she and Maximo hadn't known each other for very long. Really, she couldn't blame him for his concern.

She shrugged. "Well, I suppose we don't know for sure. If they were careless enough to give me your sample they might have been mislabeled. That would let you off the hook." The color in his face darkened and she felt instantly contrite. "I'm sorry. That was a tasteless thing to say."

"It was." He slipped his arm through hers and led her back toward their rooms. "I don't consider myself *on the hook*. I want this child."

"I only meant the marriage," she mumbled.

"The marriage should hardly be noticeable for either of us. Despite the change in location for you."

"Glad to know I won't be too heavy a ball and chain," she snapped.

"Not at all. And make no mistake, I've been married, and I'm not looking for that sort of relationship out of this." He released her arm and made his way up the stairs without her.

He had mentioned that he hadn't been planning on getting married again and up until then she had been certain it was love for his wife that kept him from wanting a new wife. Now she wasn't entirely certain.

And why should she care? He wasn't going to be her husband in any true sense of the word. He would be her partner. They would raise their baby together during the day and at night he would warm the bed of some lithe, six-foot-tall blonde. And she would go to bed alone and enjoy the solitude of her bed. And cold sheets. So why didn't that sound fair, or appealing, at all?

\* \* \*

"This is wonderful!" Isabella hadn't stopped chattering since she and Alison had gotten into the limo. "My *mamma* never allows me to go shopping."

"Your mother never lets you go shopping?" Alison couldn't imagine being controlled to such a degree. The very thought of it made her feel claustrophobic. "And are we supposed to be doing this now?"

Isabella had been very excited about taking a trip to help furnish a new, princess-worthy wardrobe for Alison, but Alison had assumed it had been Max's idea. And she certainly hadn't imagined that her future sister-in-law might be forbidden from going.

A slight blush stained Isabella's high cheekbones. "Not exactly."

Anger, not directed at Isabella, tightened her stomach. "Why aren't you allowed to shop?"

A mutinous expression creased Isabella's forehead. "Shopping is not a skill required of the future wife of a sheikh."

"You're engaged?" The other woman seemed very young to her. Naive, but very sweet.

She shrugged one very lovely shoulder. "More or less. I have an arranged marriage."

"An arranged marriage?"

It felt wrong to Alison, the thought that such a lovely, gentle person was being farmed out to a man she didn't even love. But then, wasn't that essentially what was happening with her? Except it was different for her. Isabella was clearly a romantic, and Alison had never imagined that *she* would marry for love. Anyway, Max was an honorable, handsome, decent man and any woman would be lucky to marry him.

Her own line of thinking shocked her. When had she come to think of him like that? It was ridiculous. She'd only known him for a few days. And she didn't *want* to marry him. She was only doing it because it was the right thing to do. That was all.

Isabella's eyes shone with passion now. "I thought I was entitled to experience a little something before I gave it all up for duty and honor. I just want to live a little bit of life. The life of my choosing." She took a deep breath as though she was trying to regain some composure. "But arranged marriages are normal in our family. It's just how things work. Well, except with you and Max, of course."

"Was Max and Selena's marriage arranged?" She felt a tiny twinge of guilt for digging into Maximo's past. It would have been one thing if she were really the woman he loved, if they had the sort of relationship where they shared confidences. But they didn't.

"Yes. Well, my mother met Selena after one of her shows. She was an opera singer…a very talented one. My parents had been pushing Max to settle down and start having babies. They encouraged him to pursue Selena and he did. I know he loved her, though, after a while. I could tell. So it was an arranged marriage in a way. Not like mine, though." She sighed. "I've never even met my fiancé."

Alison only half heard the rest of the conversation. She was too busy processing the information she'd just received. No wonder Maximo's view on marriage was so pragmatic. He'd made it sound as though his mother had introduced them, but she had assumed that he'd married her for love, not duty. Although Isabella was certain he'd grown to love Selena.

She was also starting to suspect that his marriage hadn't been a perfect one. She could see it in the tension that pulled up around his eyes when he spoke of his late wife. But they had been through so much as a couple, perhaps it was only natural that they would have had some strain put on the relationship.

She couldn't figure out why it all suddenly seemed so important. It just did. The more she got to know Max as a person, the more she wanted to know about him. She just wanted to…to understand him. And that was normal. He was the father of her baby; of course she wanted to understand him.

The limo pulled up to the curb of what looked like a very upscale row of boutiques. The driver opened the door and Isabella slid out. Alison followed. The ocean was only a hundred yards away from the shops, and the chilly salt air did wonders for the eternal churning in Alison's stomach. The shops were all set into small, historic stone buildings, but just at the end of the row of boutiques there was a new, massive casino. It wasn't all lit up like Vegas, rather it was more sedate, in keeping with the theme of the rest of the district. Maximo really was a genius. What he'd done to revamp the economy of his country was brilliant.

Women in expensive clothing milled around on the cobblestone walks sipping coffee that was as designer as their handbags. The men, Alison assumed, were in the casino.

"Princess Isabella!" Both Isabella and Alison turned to the sound of a man shouting. A flash went off, followed by more flashes.

Alison's eyes widened. There was a pack of people, men and women, holding cameras, They were moving toward the limo quickly, microphones and recorders held out.

"Are you Alison Whitman? Prince Maximo Rossi's

fiancée?" A woman shouted just before snapping a picture with her camera.

"Why are you getting married so quickly?"

"Does it bother you that you aren't as glamorous as his first wife?"

"Is he good in bed?"

Questions—lots of questions, inappropriate questions—were flying at her from all directions, and the paparazzi was moving in closer, crowding them up against the side of the limo.

"Back up!" Alison yelled, afraid she was about to get crushed against the side of the car. Afraid for her baby. But no one was paying attention because her statement hadn't included any hint of scandal.

Isabella managed to get the door open, and Alison slid into the car after her, closing the door and locking it behind them. "Drive!" she said, banging on the partition between the front and backseat. The princess drew a shaky hand over her face. "No wonder I'm not allowed to do this."

"That was…overwhelming," Alison said, leaning back against the seat. She hadn't expected that. Hadn't factored it in when she'd imagined being married to Max. She wanted to cry. Nothing was going like it was supposed to. Living like this was so foreign, and such a complete departure from how she'd imagined her life. It was only just now sinking in, how much she was changing her life to give her baby a father.

Isabella's expression turned sad. "It was always like that for Max and Selena. The press couldn't get enough of them."

Alison couldn't imagine how hard it must have been for them. Cameras following them all the time, the constant, insistent crush of bodies every time they went out in public. She wasn't sure she could cope with it.

*But it's your life now.*

She put her hand on her stomach and tried to calm the wild, fluttery wings of panic that were making her entire body tremble.

Isabella picked up her cell phone and punched numbers rapidly. "Max," she all but shouted into the phone. "We just got ambushed by the paparazzi."

She cast Alison a sideways glance, her expression guilty. "I wanted to go shopping. I didn't think…"

Alison could hear the muffled tirade that Max was subjecting his sister to. Isabella grimaced, but let him talk until he was through yelling. "She's fine. The baby, too, I'm sure. We'll see you in a moment."

Isabella hung up the phone. "I've never heard him sound like that before. He's worried. He must really love you."

Alison's heart squeezed and a restless, burning ache seemed to open up inside of her, one that she was desperate to have filled. But she didn't know what she needed to fill it.

That was a lie. She was starting to think she knew exactly what would fill it. But that was a something she was too scared to face. Everything seemed to be closing in on her at once; the stark reality of what all the changes becoming a princess would entail, and even more terrifying, the reality of the feelings she was starting to have for her future husband.

When they got back to the *castillo* Maximo was pacing in the vast entryway, his expression thunderous. "That was incredibly foolish and immature of you, Isabella," he ground out. "You could have both been hurt."

"I didn't know it would be like that!" Isabella protested. "How would I? I'm never allowed out anywhere!"

The fierceness in his expression diminished slightly and he blew out a hard breath. "Did you see any press badges?" he demanded, the moment they walked into the room. "If you have names I will see that the people responsible for this are thrown in jail."

Isabella shook her head. "I don't think any of them had ID on display."

"They were just doing their jobs, Max," Alison said. "There's no need to throw anyone in jail. We're fine. It was scary but they weren't trying to hurt us or anything."

"I don't tolerate that kind of gutter press in my country," he bit out. "If a reporter wants to take pictures that's fine, but there is no excuse for chasing down a couple of innocent women. Whether they intended to hurt you or not isn't the issue. They *could* have hurt you."

Alison put a hand on his arm, the need to touch him, to offer some kind of balm for his rage, was too strong for her to fight against. "We're fine. The baby is fine."

"We're leaving," he said curtly. "Until the media firestorm is over we're not staying in Turan." He pulled his phone out of his pocket and punched in a number, then barked orders in Italian to whoever was unfortunate enough to be on the other end.

He hung up and turned to face Alison. "Go and pack, *cara mia*. We're going to start our honeymoon early."

## CHAPTER SEVEN

THE flight to the island of Maris was short. The small plane touched down in a field of moss-colored grass only ten minutes after takeoff. The island itself was less mountainous than Turan, with white sand beaches that bled into expansive fields and thick olive groves.

There was no car waiting for them when they disembarked from the plane.

Maximo had spent most of the half-hour flight on his phone making arrangements for any work he needed to do to be finished remotely from the island. She'd spent the whole flight feeling shaky and...excited? No. Just shaky about the prospect of being almost alone with him in such a beautiful, isolated, romantic place.

"You were joking about the honeymoon thing, right?" she asked, surveying the vast expanse of green around them.

He turned to face her, the expression in his dark eyes so hot it burned her down to her toes. "I promised I wouldn't force you, Alison, but I didn't say I wouldn't seduce you."

Her stomach flipped, and as her nausea was starting to fade already there was no way she could place the blame on her pregnancy. "Well, that isn't...it's not...you won't be able to."

He leaned in, his lips just a breath away from hers. "What did I tell you about issuing challenges?"

"I..." She couldn't tear her eyes away from his mouth, couldn't stop herself from leaning in just slightly...

He withdrew suddenly and began to walk, as though nothing had just passed between them. As though she wasn't about to melt into a puddle of satisfied longing in the grassy field. "It's just a short walk through the grass. The villa is just through the grove." He pointed to the knot of olive trees that were directly in front of them.

They came through the brush and into a landscaped clearing with stone paths and beautifully kept gardens. A large circular fountain was at the center of the courtyard, and beyond it was the three-story villa with cream stucco walls and Spanish-tile roofing.

"It's gorgeous!" She couldn't help but think that Selena must have loved it here. It was idyllic. There were no roads, no city noises of any kind; just broad expanses of azure sky and acres of virgin land. It was the perfect escape for a couple who were desperately in love and wanted nothing more than to spend all of their time devoted only to each other. Talking, laughing, exploring, making love.

"Selena never came here."

It was as if he could read her mind sometimes, and given the recent tenor of her thoughts, that was a disquieting notion indeed.

She turned her head sharply and he laughed. "You wear your thoughts pretty openly. You looked sad. Although I can never understand why you feel so much for my late wife."

A deep sadness filled her and she felt tears sting her eyes. "It's just that...I have all that she wanted. It feels wrong somehow that I'm here with you. With the baby you both wanted. I'm the wrong woman."

He took her hand and led her to a stone bench. He sat and pulled her down gently, bringing her close to the heat of his body, her thigh touching his. "*Cara*, I don't know what the future would have held for Selena and me if she had lived. None of us can know that. But I don't think of this baby as belonging to Selena. This is *our* baby. Yours and mine."

She gave him a watery smile. "I appreciate that."

"I cannot regret it, Alison. I can't regret that you're carrying my baby, our baby. It is a dream I never thought to see realized, a child of my own. You have given that hope back to me and I can only be grateful for the mix-up at the lab now. Without it, I would not have this chance."

He put his hand over her stomach. He did that a lot now, and she had come to enjoy the gentle pressure of his touch, the tingling warmth that the contact always brought. She couldn't regret it, either. There was no way she could. She cared for Maximo, respected him. She was very glad that her baby would have him for a father.

He turned his focus from her and onto the house. "I started building the villa before her death. She was very unhappy with the location and refused to visit it. I had hoped it would be our family home. But she preferred the city."

"I'm sorry you lost her."

He shielded his eyes from the sun with his hand. "I lost her long before she died."

Again she caught that glimmer of sadness in his otherwise composed expression. And she wanted to fix it with a ferocity that shocked and scared her. "I know you were going through a hard time, but I'm sure she loved you, Max."

"She was unhappy. Being a princess demanded much more of her than she'd anticipated it would."

"But she had you."

"Sometimes. My position has always demanded that I travel a lot. Selena didn't want to be dragged around on business trips. She wanted someone to entertain her. Someone to be with her. Take care of her. She did not suffer from that same independent streak that you do," he said, the ghost of a smile touching his lips. "I can't fault her for that. I can't fault her for being unhappy."

Alison couldn't understand how Selena could have been unhappy with Maximo. There was something about him that just made her want to be with him. She liked his smell, the comforting heat of his body as he sat next to her on the bench. The way he touched her belly, so gently, reverently. Being with him made her feel secure. Happy. Cared for in a way she couldn't remember ever being cared for.

The realization was enough to shock her into standing from the bench. She was starting to need him too much. Even without sex and romance he was burrowing under her skin. Yes, Maximo was a good man, but he was also an arrogant autocrat who expected her to just fall in line and do exactly as he said. When he said marriage was the only option he expected her to see it his way, and when he said they were going on an early honeymoon she'd found herself on a plane within five minutes of his edict.

It was far too easy to forget all of that when he turned on his charm and flashed that sexy smile at her. But she wasn't going to let herself do that anymore. It was too dangerous.

"I'm hot. I want to go inside," she said.

Maximo didn't know what had caused the dramatic shift in Alison's mood. She had been sweet one moment, not resisting his attempts to touch her, and then she had gone stiff and jumped as far away from him as she could manage in one movement.

He wanted her. He had been totally honest about his intention to seduce her, and he did intend to. He was going to make this advanced honeymoon a honeymoon in the most basic sense of the word. He ached for her every night as he lay in his empty bed, images of her fiery hair spread around her head as he laid her back onto his pillows. That gorgeous mouth parted on a sigh as he sank into her willing body…

His need for her was so strong, so intense that his entire body ached with it. Desire on this level was a madness he'd never before experienced. And it was an ideal scenario for it. Alison did not want love, but he knew she felt the same kind of lust for him that he felt for her. Lust he could handle. Love was not on the agenda.

This feeling, this overwhelming passion, was about as far removed from love as anything he could think of. But then, Alison was as far removed from Selena as one woman could possibly be from another. And for that he was grateful. Alison was fiery, independent. When she was angry with him, as she seemed to be, inexplicably, at the moment, she let him know.

Selena had been so delicate. She had needed him, needed his protection, his support. He had failed at that. Failed spectacularly. In the end she'd withdrawn from him completely and he'd had no way to reach her, no way to stanch the flow of grief that had seemed to flow endlessly inside of her.

At least with Alison it would be different. He wouldn't be caught in that same, endless hell his first marriage had been in the end. She wouldn't cling to him, expect him to solve all of her problems then blame him for everything that seemed to go wrong.

Guilt struck him low and fast. Yes, Selena had been difficult at times, but hadn't it been his job to slay her dragons? Even if there had been more dragons in her life than there were in most people's, that was irrelevant. She had been his wife. It had been his job to make her happy. He had failed.

But with Alison at least he could stay out of those murky waters. Alison didn't want a real marriage relationship and neither did he. They had that in common. And, whether she wanted to admit it or not, they also shared an attraction.

He stood and moved to follow her into the villa, banishing all thoughts of his first marriage as he watched the gentle sway of Alison's hips as she walked ahead of him.

Oh, yes, he was going to enjoy the seduction of his fiancée very much.

Maximo was in his private office, giving Alison a chance to sleep off the afternoon's stress. She was tired. She needed to rest. That was the refrain he kept replaying in his mind, when his body was demanding that he find her immediately and commence with his seduction plan.

He'd been trying to concentrate on work, trying not to focus on the woman sleeping down the hall. But it was a useless endeavor. His desire for Alison was slowly taking him over; an almost primitive need that seemed bone deep, as though it was in him, inseparable from him now.

He was almost ready to give up on his attempt at productivity when his mobile phone rang. It was his personal physician calling with the test results.

The call took only a minute, and in that minute his life was changed.

# CHAPTER EIGHT

MAXIMO opened the door to Alison's bedroom without knocking. She was asleep and her beauty stole his breath, made him feel weak with desire, like a starving man in desperate need of nourishment. Even with all of the turmoil inside of him, he still wanted her.

"Alison." He sat down on the bed and took her hand in his. "Alison." He moved his other hand over her face, brushed her hair back. She stirred beneath his touch, her body arching, a soft sigh escaping her lips.

His body hardened instantly, his stomach tightening. "Wake up, Alison."

She rubbed her hand over her eyes and rolled to the side, her coppery eyes cloudy with sleep, her hair tousled. And he had never seen a more beautiful woman. She was so beautiful it made him ache.

"Max?" his name on her lips, her voice thick with sleep, was the single most arousing thing he'd ever heard in his life.

"The doctor called."

She sat up quickly, pushing her hair back. "What did she say?" The film of tears in her eyes made his heart feel too large for his chest.

"I'm not a carrier. There isn't a chance our baby will have Cystic Fibrosis."

A short cry escaped her lips and she threw her arms around his neck, sobs shaking her frame. He held her close and let her release all of her emotion, let her do it for both of them. He held her until his neck was wet with her tears.

"I was so afraid," she whispered, her lips brushing his jaw. "I thought… I didn't want to watch our child die, Max."

"You won't have to."

"My sister was so young when it took her. It was horrible. It killed me to see it happen to her, to watch her just get weaker. I couldn't have gone through it with our baby."

His heart burned for her, her pain so real, so much a part of him, that he felt it all the way in his bones. "I didn't know you'd been through that."

"That was why…" She took a gulp of air. "That was why it was so important to me to know. I needed to prepare myself. I couldn't just be blindsided with something like that. I don't know if there would ever have been a way to be really prepared for it…but knowing now. Oh, it's such a relief."

She pulled back and started to wipe the moisture from her tearstained face. Her nose was red, her eyes swollen, and still he wanted her so much it was physically painful to hold himself back. Seeing the intensity of her love for their child only increased his desire for her.

He cupped the back of her head, stroking his thumb over her silky, strawberry locks. "No matter what, we would have made it. There's no way we could love our baby more or less than we do. But I'm very glad that we don't have to worry about that."

"Me, too."

Her arms were still linked around his neck and she very slowly moved her hands so that her fingers were twined through his hair. She moved them slowly, sliding them through, her touch sending shock waves of hot pleasure rippling through him. It was such a simple touch. In general he would have said there wasn't anything erotic about it. Except in this moment, with this woman, it was the single most erotic sensation he could ever remember feeling.

She leaned in slightly, her eyelids lowering, her lashes fanning over her cheeks. Her mouth was so close to his that one slight movement would join them together. But he wanted her to do it. Wanted her to make the move.

"Max, I don't really know what I'm doing here, but I don't know if I can stop myself, either," she whispered, her breath hot and sweet against his lips.

Then she closed the distance between them, settling her lips over his, her kiss tentative, almost shy. It was strange because there was nothing insecure or shy about Alison, and yet she kissed almost as if she was an innocent. Not that he could claim personal experience in that area.

When the tip of her tongue touched his lower lip his control snapped completely. He growled, deepening the kiss, sliding his tongue against hers. She parted her lips for him, granting him access, her feminine moan of pleasure tightening his gut, increasing his arousal.

He slowly pressed her down on the bed. She arched her back, rubbing her breasts against his chest. They had too many clothes on. He needed her naked. He needed to be naked. To be able to slide inside of her, and finally purge himself of the almost surreal level of desire he felt for her.

He moved his hands over her curves, cupped her

breasts, teased the hardened points of her nipples. He could come just touching her, even through her clothes. Never, not even when he'd been a teenage virgin, had a woman ever tested his self-control like this.

"Wait," she said, rolling away from him, her eyes wide. "I don't… I can't…" Her breathing was ragged, her lips swollen. "I can't."

"Why is it that you can't all of a sudden? You want this—I know you do."

"I don't," she said, her breathing ragged. "I'm sorry. We…it would be better if we were just friends. What would happen if this—" she gestured to the air between them "—didn't work out? Then we would be bitter divorcés shuttling our child back and forth and sharing holidays. But if we just keep it platonic then things would be simpler. It's the smartest thing to do."

"I have no trouble keeping my commitments. When I speak my vows to you I will mean them. If you see divorce in our future it will not be me that's instigated it."

Alison forked her shaking fingers in her hair. "Well, I have no intention of divorcing you, but when you introduce sex into a relationship it complicates things."

Maximo stood up from the bed, not bothering to hide the thick length of his erection that was pressing against the front of his slacks. "Things are already complicated by the attraction between us. Sex would only alleviate some of the tension."

He turned and walked out of the room. Alison cursed out loud to the empty room. Why had she done that? Why had she kissed him like a sex-starved maniac?

*And why did you stop him?* That was the question her body was asking. She was so hot for him, wet for him, needy for him. His kiss had totally stolen every ounce of her control. She'd been ready to let him do anything he wanted with her, to her. She'd craved the loss of control, the descent into blissful oblivion at his hands.

And in the end that was what had jarred her back to reality. The feelings inside of her had gone so far beyond just a simple case of lust. And she couldn't deal with that. She just couldn't.

She didn't want to fall in love. She liked Maximo too much already and if she gave into her desire for him what would keep her from falling all the way? Nothing. She was too dangerously close to love already to take the chance.

In that moment when he'd told her that the test was negative she'd just wanted to cling to him, and it had been so easy to imagine that their relationship was real, and that they were a real couple, drawing support and strength from each other.

But that wasn't the case. They were just two strangers thrown together, making the most out of a crazy situation. He had his life, she had hers, and together they had the baby. But that was all that linked them.

Maximo had said he wouldn't divorce her, and maybe he wouldn't. No matter what he would never abandon her baby.

He'd been faithful to Selena, but he'd loved Selena. Without love what was going to keep him interested in her? When she gained baby weight and got stretch marks, what would make her more interesting, more attractive than other women? And he could certainly have any woman he wanted.

There was no way, no way at all, that she was going to set herself up for that.

And if she had to spend the rest of her days achy and

physically unsatisfied it would be a small price to pay to keep her soul from being irrevocably shattered.

Over the course of the next three weeks Maximo broke his promise to her. Oh, he never once tried to force himself on her, not that she had ever believed he would, but he didn't try to seduce her, either. And some small, confused part of her was disappointed that he seemed to have accepted that she truly didn't want a sexual relationship with him.

Now that he'd come to that conclusion she lay awake every night, her body on fire, her mind replaying snatches of every encounter she'd ever had with him. And then adding some more interesting things.

In her mind they hadn't stopped the day they'd found out the test results. No, in her fantasies she had kept kissing him, had unbuttoned his shirt to reveal the hard muscles and golden skin she knew lay underneath. And he'd done the same to her: unbuttoned her shirt, flicked open the clasp of her bra and then he'd lower his head and take one tightened bud into his mouth…

Alison snapped the laptop she'd been using shut and stood abruptly. It was the computer Max had given her to establish contacts at the Cystic Fibrosis Foundation. She and Max had discussed getting a Turani branch established after they'd found out the test results, and he'd given her the task of getting it mobilized. She didn't really like doing all of the work over the Internet, but it had been better than just sitting around wallowing in her lust for the man she couldn't, wouldn't, let herself have.

Maximo had been nice enough to provide her with a computer, and a staggering budget. He'd also given her the use of an empty bedroom that had been converted into an office. The windows faced the ocean, the bright crystalline water offering her at least a modicum of stress relief, even if it could not take away the hunger that constantly gnawed at her.

It was getting so bad that she was starting to wonder exactly why she was denying herself what she so desperately wanted.

*Imminent heartbreak, possible abandonment, the loss of all of your independence and hard-earned self-worth!*

Her practical self remembered all of the reasons. It was the wanton little hussy that had control over her erogenous zones that seemed to forget.

Thankfully her morning sickness had abated. If she couldn't have some measure of relief from the constant arousal that kept her in a perpetual state of heightened awareness, then at least she wasn't also spending most of the morning with her head in the toilet.

Even now she felt restless, her body humming just from the knowledge that Maximo was down the hall working in his own office.

He'd been so good to her since they'd come to the island. He'd been kind and attentive and taken care of anything she could possibly need. He was playing the part of doting, but platonic, fiancé just perfectly. It was as if he was doing it on purpose to make her life miserable.

She stretched and tried to shake off the electric feeling of arousal that seemed to have attached itself to her every nerve ending. Her skin felt as if it was too tight for her body, and everything inside of her felt as if it might jump out and escape at any moment.

What she needed was some physical exertion. Badly. She'd been feeling so awful since she'd gotten pregnant that she hadn't worked out at all. Maybe that was why she felt so jittery. She'd had no outlet for her energy; none of the release that a good bout of exercise always gave her.

It was way too easy to imagine ways she and Max might find some physical release together.

Walking out of the office and down the hall to her room, she made the decision to get out of the house and get some air. Maybe breathing in the stale atmosphere of the villa was chipping away at her common sense. Except the villa smelled wonderful and there was nothing stale about it, but hey, a girl needed her excuses.

She rifled through her belongings until she found a swimsuit that Maximo had had sent over to Maris a few days after they'd arrived. It was brief…shockingly so. The black, stretchy fabric didn't have enough yardage to swaddle a newborn, and yet it was intended to cover a grown woman's curves. And hers had only become more ample as her pregnancy progressed.

Her breasts were always a little full for her petite frame, but now they just made everything she wore seem indecent. The swimsuit was an extreme example of that.

She tried to ignore her reflection in the mirror, tried not to focus on her pale flesh spilling over the midnight fabric of the miniscule top. Sighing, she grabbed a towel and wrapped it firmly around herself, hiding her new, extra-lush curves and her burgeoning tummy, before padding down to the large Olympic-size pool.

Thankfully the pool area, like the rest of the villa, and the rest of the island, was extremely private. Large flowering bushes had been planted around the perimeter of the pool, just high enough to guard against curious eyes, but low enough to leave the view of the ocean visible.

Alison slid beneath the surface of the water, sighing as its coolness washed over her heated skin. She began to swim laps, reveling in the chance to burn off some of her restless energy. To let her mind go blank so that she could just forget about Maximo, even just for a moment.

When she reached the edge of the pool she gripped the cement lip, wiping the droplets of water from her face.

"You swim well."

A sensual shiver shot through the length of her body. Would that voice never stop affecting her this way? Would she ever be able to just find Maximo's presence… boring? Every day?

She looked up, her eyes widening as she took in the muscular legs, partially revealed by his board shorts, and, her eyes widened further, the broad expanse of his well-defined chest.

"Thank you," she said tightly, swimming away from that end up the pool and moving to the ladder that hung over the side. "I was on the team in high school." She climbed out of the water and grabbed her towel quickly, trying to cover the acres of bare skin that were on display thanks to her ridiculous swimsuit.

She turned to face him and her eyes were immediately drawn back to his superbly masculine chest. Good Lord, but he was one hot man. All hard muscle with just the right amount of dark chest hair sprinkled over his golden skin. Just enough to remind her how much of a man he was. As if she needed reminding. What she needed was to forget.

"So you swam in high school?"

She nodded, sitting on the lounger chair that was positioned beneath a palm tree shading the patio area. "I did a lot of things in high school. Swimming. The debate team. I worked on the school newspaper. Anything and everything to earn extra credit."

"Let me guess…you had a 4.0 GPA?"

She shrugged. "I was capable of it so anything less would have been a failure. I needed to earn scholarships so that I could go to school."

"Your parents didn't offer to pay for your schooling?" He crossed his arms over his chest, the motion creating a fascinating play of muscle that she was powerless to look away from.

"My mother couldn't have afforded it. When my…" She didn't know why she was telling him anything, and yet it seemed so easy to talk to him. She wanted to talk to him, wanted to keep him there with her. She cleared her throat. "When my father left things became difficult for us financially. My mother didn't have the means, or the drive, to earn a living for us."

He lowered his dark eyebrows and rubbed a hand over his jaw, his skin rasping against the black stubble that was starting to grow. "Your father didn't pay child support?"

"We didn't even know where he was. He walked out the door one day and never came back. I haven't heard from him in fifteen years."

"That must have been hard."

"Yes. It was harder for my mother, though. She just kind of self-destructed after he left. Kimberly was gone, and then Dad was, too, and she just didn't seem to have it in her to keep going. So she sank instead. She nearly took me with her."

He sat in the chair next to hers and leaned close, the

musky scent of him teasing her senses. "Is that why you're so independent?"

"I had to be. People aren't going to take care of you—they're going to take care of themselves. I just learned that at an earlier age than some. But I survived. I made my own way. My own success."

"But there is no shame in accepting help from others."

"That's quite something coming from you. When was the last time you accepted help?"

A slow smile curved his lips. "I can't remember."

"I didn't think so."

"But some people need more help than others," he said, a shadow passing over his face for a moment.

"I don't believe that. Some people wallow rather than moving forward."

"Is that what you think? That your mother should have tried harder?"

She nodded emphatically. "Yes. That's what I think. You can't just self-destruct because somebody leaves you in the lurch. It's never a good idea to depend on someone like that. You become so accustomed to leaning on them that you get weak, and then when they leave, when they fail you, you won't be able to stand on your own anymore because you've lost all of your own strength. And everybody fails at some point."

His eyes darkened. "Yes. And some damage is irreparable."

"Yes," she said softly, thinking of the void left by Kimberly, by her father and then, even though she'd still been there physically, by her mother. "That's why I don't need people."

"Don't you?"

"No. I earn my own living. I've achieved my goals on my own, without help from anyone. I don't do need."

"Neither do I," he said, his voice growing thicker, deeper. "And yet, something about you…" He took her hand and placed it on his bare chest, the heat of his skin singeing her fingers, his heartbeat raging against her palm. "Something about this feels a lot like need."

She sucked in a breath. She couldn't deny it. Her own body was on fire with response to his. Her heart pounding in time with his, her nipples beading, aching, slick moisture dampening her core.

"That's why we can't," she said bleakly, trying to pull her hand away, but he gripped it with his, held it tightly against the hard wall of his chest.

"And you think if we deny it, that it will go away? Has it faded at all in the past three weeks for you? Because I have been spending all of my nights dreaming of you. Of making love to you, touching your soft skin, thrusting into your beautiful body."

Heat coursed through her and she knew her cheeks were bright red, but not from embarrassment. Well, not only from embarrassment, although his frank description of what he wanted to do with her was a little bit beyond her experience level. But the heat was from desire, the fierce pulse of it that pounded through her and made her limbs feel weak, made her feel as if she could be reckless. Like she could grab what she wanted with both hands and forget that such a thing as consequences even existed.

He leaned in, his mouth covering hers, his tongue parting her lips expertly. She didn't hesitate. She opened to him, let her tongue tangle with his, wrapped her arms around his neck so that he could kiss her harder, deeper.

His hands deftly worked at the knots on her bikini top and before she realized what was happening the fabric had slipped away, leaving her breasts bare to him. She arched against his chest, the slight dusting of hair that covered his skin lightly abrading her nipples. The coarse friction sent a wave of sensation washing through her body, making her internal muscles clench in anticipation of his touch. His possession. She squirmed, trying to find some way to alleviate the hollow ache that was slowly taking over her body. She knew it wasn't going to work, that whatever she did, even if it brought her to orgasm, wasn't going to satisfy her. Because she wasn't going to be satisfied until their bodies were joined together, until he was filling that void.

He lowered his dark head and she watched, completely spellbound as he sucked one pink nipple into his mouth, his tongue working the sensitized tip. She let her head fall back, let a loud moan escape her lips. She was past the point of caring about what noises she made, past the point of caring about anything except for this. Maximo. His touch. His wicked mouth doing such wonderful, shocking things to her.

"You're so beautiful," he said thickly before lowering his head and drawing her other nipple into his mouth. He released her, laving her with the flat of his tongue before scattering kisses over her breasts, her collarbone, down to her belly button and back up again.

She was on fire, dying for him, all remnants of control long since thrown out the window. She couldn't think when he was kissing her. Couldn't plan. Couldn't do anything except revel in the things he, and only he, could do to her.

Would it have been like this with any man? If she

had given someone the chance sooner would they have lit her body on fire, too?

No. She knew that instinctively. She didn't need a vast amount of experience to know that this wasn't everyday garden-variety attraction. This was something much hotter, something much more lethal. And she was willingly partaking in it, even knowing how potentially deadly it was.

She felt the hard evidence of his arousal against her thigh and she moved her hand down, pressed her palm against his firm length and squeezed him gently.

A short curse fell from his lips and he captured her mouth again, bucking his hips against her hand, his control obviously as shredded as her own. She squeezed him again and she reveled in the low growl that rumbled in his chest. Always before when she'd imagined being intimate with a man, she'd imagined it meant giving him power over her. But what she hadn't realized was just how much power *she* would have over him.

She moved her hand over the length of him, not quite able to believe just how thick and hard he felt. She hadn't realized that men could be so big. And yet, there was no fear with that revelation, only a sensual thrill that rushed through her, making her feel light-headed, breathless.

Dimly Alison registered the chirpy tones of a cell phone. Despite the interruption, her hands continued to roam over him, to explore him, the everyday sound not quite able to penetrate the fog of desire that was totally clouding her ability for rational thought.

*"Che cavolo."* Max swore and jumped away from her as though her touch burned him. He moved to the table where he'd placed his mobile phone and answered it in rough Italian, his chest rising and falling harshly with

his breathing, the aggressive jut of his arousal pushing visibly against the thin fabric of his shorts.

Alison's heart was pounding hard in her ears. Very slowly she started to come back to reality. She could feel the heat of the sun, the salt breeze…hear seagulls screaming at each other down on the beach. She had just about made love with a man outside. Correction: she had been in the process of making love with him even if they hadn't been quite to the point of actual intercourse. And any of the household staff members could have come out and seen them, caught them in the act.

She crossed her arms over her breasts, acutely aware of her nudity. Before it had seemed freeing, so nice not to have anything between her and Max. Now it just seemed embarrassing. She didn't feel sexy anymore. She just felt bare, exposed.

She fished her swimsuit top from beneath the chair and turned her back to Maximo, who was still engaged in his phone conversation, tying her top back on with shaking hands, her clumsy fingers taking twice as long to get herself covered again. She picked up the towel and knotted it fiercely at her breasts, craving all the cover she could get. She took advantage of Maximo's distraction and sneaked quietly back into the villa. She was not hanging around for another postmortem on an aborted make-out session.

More importantly, she wasn't going to risk being there if he wanted to pick up where they left off because, despite the healthy dose of humiliation she was suffering from, she wasn't certain she would be able to resist him.

# CHAPTER NINE

MAXIMO got off the phone with the casino manager and cursed. Not because the problem at the casino hadn't been easy to solve—that issue had been handled in only a few minutes—but because of the unsatisfied desire that was still raging through him.

He couldn't believe he'd almost had sex with Alison outside by his pool, with all of the speed and finesse of a very horny schoolboy. He had never, ever lost control with a woman like that before. He had always taken time when romancing a woman. Selena had never wanted it any other way. She had always needed candles, a dimly lit room. He had always spent at least an hour arousing her body before he'd even considered taking things to their natural conclusion.

But with Alison there had been no romance, no candles. He'd been ready to plunge into her without a full five minutes of foreplay. And what foreplay there had been was clumsy, driven by an intense need, not any kind of skill or consideration. He didn't know this part of himself; the part that only Alison seemed to be able to bring out in him.

He was a man who prized his control. He always thought things through, always led first with his mind before jumping into action. And yet, Alison, his beautiful, bewitching fiancée, the woman who was pregnant with his child, robbed him of his ability to think coherently.

It was the unknown that was causing his body to respond this way. It had to be. He had desired her from the first moment he'd seen her and every night since then he'd dreamed of her, her smell, the touch of her soft hands, and the wet press of her lips over his body. There was no way the fantasy would live up to the reality, though, because it never did.

He needed to take her, to know once and for all what her desire for him would taste like, know what it felt like to be inside her, know what sounds she would make when he brought her to completion. And once the mystery was solved, the edge would be worn away. It had to be.

He couldn't wait anymore. He wanted her, and he knew for certain that she wanted him with the same ferocity, that she was just as hungry as he was. And he wasn't going to allow her to deny it any longer.

Alison scrubbed the chlorine from her skin and wished she could wash away the imprint from Maximo's touch half as easily. No such luck. Even with the scalding water from the shower coursing over her body, she could still feel the impression of where his hands had touched her, teased her, where his mouth had seared her. She shivered despite the heat and shut the water off.

During her shower she'd decided that she wasn't ashamed of what she'd done with Max. She was entitled to sexual pleasure if she wanted it. And that was a massive admission in and of itself. She *was* embarrassed, though, because she'd totally lost track of time and place, and anyone could have walked right up to them and she would have been much too lost in what they were doing to notice. Maybe Maximo, with his stable of previous lovers, was sophisticated enough to deal with something like that. He could probably turn it into a saucy anecdote and laugh about it with his sophisticated friends. Not her, though. She just didn't have the experience for that, which just went to prove how out of her league Max was.

Ashamed as she was to admit it, she'd looked him up when she'd been on the computer in the office, and she'd seen the kind of women he'd had in his life. Even before his marriage to the supernaturally lovely Selena, he'd had a very high taste level where his girlfriends were concerned. All of them were high-profile models, actresses, socialites, and all of them had been tall, thin and gorgeous. They weren't the kind of women to run and hide from sexual attraction. They were the kind of women who would pounce on it and tame it, take what they wanted and enjoy doing it.

She realized that she was clenching her fists so tightly that her knuckles were white and she slowly released them.

She'd never considered herself a coward. On the contrary, she'd always been prideful about how brave she thought she was. Brave and sensible. Sensible enough to protect herself, keep herself from coming unraveled and completely dependent on someone. Brave because she'd gone out and learned to stand on her own feet, made things happen for herself.

And she'd been the biggest, delusional idiot.

She'd been a coward. She hadn't dealt with anything. She'd completely walled off a portion of herself so she wouldn't have to deal with all of the complications that might result from a relationship.

She'd denied any sort of desire for companionship, totally squashed her sexuality, and all the while she'd been congratulating herself for being so strong. It wasn't strength that had led her to do those things, it was fear. And that was a bitter pill to swallow. She wasn't much better than her mother. It was just that her general wariness was preemptive rather than a response to something that had happened to her. The result, however, was much the same. Oh, she might not subject everyone to lengthy, vitriolic speeches about men and how you couldn't trust them, but she carried that belief inside of her. If she wasn't careful it was going to poison her.

It had to change. She was crippling herself. Ironic, since she'd always been so terrified that losing a lover would do that to her, and she'd done it to herself.

She wasn't ready to rush headlong into falling in love, but maybe…

Maybe she could fulfill her desire for Max. Those women in the magazines, the women who had dated Max before his marriage, knew that sex wasn't love. Knew it and reveled in it. They didn't suppress that part of themselves, not like she had done for so long.

She exited the bathroom and went into her connecting bedroom, sinking onto the bed, holding her towel tightly around her naked body. She was such a hopeless case for Max that even the rough abrasion of the terry cloth over her bare skin was turning her on.

It had always been easy to act aloof around men. She hadn't really wanted any of them. There had been a few times when she'd really liked someone, felt a kind of bitter melancholy over not pursuing anything serious with them. But this, what she felt for Max, was a consuming hunger that was with her all the time. A spark that smoldered in her belly, ready to burst into flame when Max so much as looked at her.

The fact that they were engaged to be married, that they were having a baby together, was the biggest thing holding her back. If she could just indulge in a fling with him, one night of passion maybe, just so she could experience it, so she could exorcise this thing that had flared so strongly between them, then she would more than happily jump into bed with him.

But the fact remained that they were engaged, and they were having a baby. And those were very, very permanent ties.

But her body was still screaming for the release she knew only Maximo would be able to give. She just didn't know if she could fight it anymore. Or if she even wanted to…

She stood from the bed and crossed to the massive closet on the other side of the room. It was packed full of designer clothing, all chosen by a personal shopper without Alison present, since the paparazzi had made shopping an impossibility. Every last article was beautiful, and a lot more revealing than anything she would have chosen for herself.

Sliding her hands over the fabrics she stopped at a midnight-blue silk dress with a low halter neckline and a floaty, knee-skimming hem. It was an extremely sexy dress, one she'd privately vowed never to wear as she'd hung it up in the closet. But now…now it seemed perfect.

She pulled it out quickly before any doubts or fears could invade and talk her out of it. She hadn't known what she was planning until that moment, but, even though she might think she was stupid in the morning, she was committed. She was going to seduce Prince Maximo Rossi.

The glow of the candlelight bathed Alison's skin in golden warmth. And there was a lot of bare skin on display. Her barely-there midnight-blue satin gown clung to her every curve and showed off the swell of her breasts, her lovely shoulders, her perfect legs. And when Maximo had pulled her chair out for her and she'd turned to look before sitting, he'd been unable to tear his gaze away from her perfect, rounded derriere.

Dinner had been an exercise in torture. She had savored every bite that she'd put in her mouth, making sensual, delighted noises and darting her slick pink tongue out to catch any flavor that had lingered on her lips. He wanted her. More than he could remember wanting any other woman in his entire life. And she wanted him, too. Yet something was stopping her from taking the final step.

She certainly didn't kiss like an inexperienced woman; she kissed like a woman with highly developed passions, a woman who knew what she wanted, knew what her lover would want. And yet she seemed to take sex very seriously. Or at least the prospect of heartbreak. But Maximo knew from experience that there were some women who simply couldn't divorce sex from love. Perhaps the idea of sleeping with a man simply because she desired him was something she was having trouble coming to terms with. But then, she was the one who claimed she hadn't been interested in love and relationships, and he couldn't imagine that she'd been planning on living a celibate existence. She was far too sexy, far too sexual, for that.

He nearly groaned out loud when she lifted her dessert spoon to her lips and licked the last remnant of chocolate from the silver surface, her pink tongue so tempting, so provocative that he could have almost found his release just watching her work the spoon in that slow, sensual way. It was way too easy to imagine that tongue on his bare skin.

"What's your stance on love?" she asked, lowering the spoon and setting it on the table.

"I've been in love. I don't believe I'll ever love anyone besides my…Selena. I don't want to love anyone else." Not because he was so attached to her memory, but because nothing about it had been worth the pain he'd endured. He'd lost Selena several times over. In the end, an impenetrable wall had gone up between them, and he hadn't been able to reach her anymore. He hadn't been able to protect her, from her grief, from death. He had no desire to ever go through that kind of hell again.

"So you don't think you're going to meet someone else?" she asked, her copper eyes deadly serious.

"I'm marrying you. You're the only 'someone else' there's going to be."

"But if you *did* want someone else would you tell me?"

"I won't."

"But if you did," she persisted, "would you tell me? I don't want to be played for a fool, Max, and I really don't want to be cheated on."

"I would tell you. You have my word that, if we were to enter into a physical relationship, I would never even entertain the thought of being unfaithful to you."

"I've been thinking a lot about what happened by the pool," she said slowly.

Tension knotted his muscles and the fire in his stomach was starting to rage out of control.

She raised her eyes to meet his and he was struck by how dark they'd gotten. She was aroused. He was definitely familiar with the signs, and his own body was more than ready to take hers up on its blatant offer.

"I want to make love," she said, her voice steady. If he hadn't spotted the slight tremor in her delicate hands he would have never known she was nervous.

"You wanted to make love by the pool. You wanted to make love that day in your room. In fact, you wanted to make love that first day in Turan, but you pulled back every time."

"I know. But I've had a lot of time to think about it." She rose from her chair, moved to stand in front of him, then leaned in and he was transfixed by her beauty, by the clear, pale skin of her flawless face, by the creamy swells of her breasts spilling over the skimpy neckline of her dress. Splaying her hands over his chest she explored him, ran her fingertips over his muscles. He sucked in a sharp breath, his body so close to the edge he was in danger of going right over.

"I want you," she said softly, leaning in and pressing her lips against his. He let her control the kiss, let her explore his mouth slowly, her tongue moving tentatively over the seam of his lips. When they separated she was panting, and he realized he was, too. "I trust you. I'm certain of that now."

"And you needed to trust me?" he asked, running his fingers through her silken, strawberry hair, reveling in her softness, her femininity.

"Yes. The attraction between us is so strong… I've never felt this way before and it scared me. It still scares me. But now I know you aren't going to use it against me."

"I'm not going to fall in love with you, either," he said roughly, hating himself for needing to be honest, especially if it might make her change her mind again.

"I know. I don't want to fall in love with you, either. But I do want your respect. I wanted to make sure you weren't just going to play with me, and no one wants to get cheated on, or abandoned."

He cupped her chin. "I swear to you that I will never leave you. And I will never humiliate you, or disrespect you, by taking another woman into our bed."

"I believe you."

She sank onto his lap and twined her arms around his neck, threading her fingers through his hair. "My whole body aches for you," she said, meeting his eyes.

"Mine, too," he said, taking her hand and placing it over his erection, showing her how much he wanted her. She moved her hand over his length, her expression so full of awe that he couldn't help but take stupid masculine pride in it.

"I think we should take this upstairs."

"The table looks fine to me," he growled, not knowing where this feral, uncivilized desire came from, not knowing what he could do to control it. She revealed something inside of him he hadn't known existed. And he didn't want to tame it; he wanted to unleash it.

"One of the staff could come in," she said breathlessly.

He pressed a kiss to the elegant line of her neck. "Now *that* we don't want. This is definitely a two-person party." He nuzzled the tender spot just beneath her earlobe and reveled in the feminine sigh of pleasure she rewarded him with. She was so eager, so responsive, and he loved it.

Alison slid from his lap, her heart pounding wildly. She'd done it. She'd committed to doing this. And she wasn't sorry for it at all. She wanted him. Needed him in a way that shocked and terrified her. She didn't know this wild, wanton version of herself. She felt as if she could do anything with him, could let him do anything to her. She trusted him with her body, wholly and completely, and the prospect of doing that only excited her.

As he stood from the chair and took her hand, his eyes burning with erotic intent, she wished, for the first time in her life, that she'd had sex with someone at some point, just so she wasn't going into this blind. Maximo had lots of experience—she'd seen the evidence of that thanks to the photos of the parade of women he'd dated in his early twenties, and he'd been married for seven years. She didn't even have a lot of kissing experience to recommend her.

On the other hand, he would make it good for her. He would know what he was doing. At her age, after having received exams from gynecologists and OBs and having the artificial insemination done she doubted there would be much of a barrier for him to deal with, if there was one at all. And that, coupled with all of his experience, would probably lessen any discomfort she might feel. And, with any luck, he might not notice.

She nearly laughed at that thought. Of course he would notice her inexperience. There was no way she was going to be able to fake some kind of blasé sophistication. Not when his touch just about melted her.

But his hand felt so good, so warm encircling hers that it was hard to care too much. He held on to her as he led her up the stairs, took her to his bedroom. There was no turning back now. And she didn't want to.

"Alison." He closed the door behind them and pulled her to him, bringing her up hard against his masculine chest. She spread her hands over his pecs, running them down his flat stomach, feeling the ridges of his ab muscles through his shirt. She'd never explored a man's body like this before, never took the time to appreciate all of the delicious differences between men and women.

He kissed her again, his mouth hard on hers, and she parted her lips willingly, meeting each thrust of his tongue with her own. He slid his hands over the silken material of her dress, over the curve of her buttocks and down her thighs. He gripped the hem of the skirt and began to pull it up slowly, bunching the slippery fabric in his hands until he had it drawn up to her waist. He moved one hand down over her rear end again and he groaned when his hand touched bare skin. His obvious appreciation thrilled her, and combined with his touch sent a shock wave of need rocketing through her.

He released her dress, keeping his hands beneath the fabric. He gripped the sides of her thong panties and dragged them down, kneeling before her on the floor as he removed them. She lifted one foot to step out of her underwear and wobbled slightly, but he steadied her by holding tightly to her hips.

He leaned in, his breath hot against the silk fabric as his mouth hovered over her slightly rounded stomach. "So beautiful." He laid his palm flat against her belly, the expression on his face so reverent, so awed, that it made her throat tighten with emotion. He leaned in and kissed her there, and she felt as if her knees would have buckled if she hadn't been held firmly in his strong grip.

Standing again he kissed her lips, her neck, her collarbone. She wasn't even aware that they'd been moving until the back of her knees came into contact with the edge of the bed. He lowered her slowly to the soft surface, his hard length brushing her hip as he joined her on the mattress.

"You're so beautiful," he said, reaching around and untying the flimsy knot that held the halter top of her dress in place. He pushed the fabric aside and revealed her breasts.

He'd seen her before, out at the pool, and already knowing that he liked the way she looked bolstered her confidence. He cupped her breasts, teased the aroused tips. She tilted her head back onto the pillow and just enjoyed his touch, relished the knot of arousal that was tightening in her pelvis. She could just stay like this forever, with him caressing her, lavishing attention on her body.

She let out a moan of disappointment when he abandoned her breasts, his hands skimming over her curves, still clothed in the thin silk of the dress. He pushed the fabric up again and exposed her naked body to his gaze. She hadn't been embarrassed for him to see her breasts, but having him so close to a part of her only her doctor had ever seen had her blushing hotly.

"Max." She was about to ask him to turn the bedroom light off, but the warm press of his lips on her thigh stalled the words. And when he parted her legs and ran his tongue along her inner thigh she lost her command of the English language entirely.

She fought to regain some control, some kind of command over her senses. Impossible when she felt as if all of the feeling inside her were too big to be contained by her skin, when she was certain she might shatter into a million pieces. A needy moan escaped her lips and her body trembled as he moved closer to the place where she was wet and aching for him. She didn't have control anymore; she felt as if she might fall from the earth and float away, as if there was nothing holding her to the bed.

She gripped the sheets, tried to focus, tried to find some shred of sanity, because this, what he was doing to her, making her feel, was terrifying. She couldn't temper it, couldn't lead it, or plan it. But she felt her hold slipping, felt herself ready to plunge over the edge, and if that happened she was afraid she would go on falling forever.

"Let go, Alison," he growled, pressing a hot kiss just above her feminine mound. "I want to make you lose control."

She shook her head, even though she knew he couldn't see. "No."

"Yes. I want you to stop thinking. I want you to feel." He ran his tongue over her flesh, flicked it over the sensitive bundle of nerves and continued down, dipping inside of her. Her hips came off the bed and he gripped them tight, holding her to him, not letting her escape. "I want you to come for me."

He continued his intimate assault, pleasuring her with his lips, his tongue, as he whispered exciting, erotic words. He pushed one finger into her tight passage and moved it in rhythm with his tongue.

A moan rose in her throat and she couldn't do anything to stop the needy sound from escaping.

"That's right, Alison," he whispered. "Let go. You can let go. I've got you."

Her mind blanked, all thoughts of control, all of her worries, falling away. And she really could only feel.

She felt as if she was reaching for something, something beautiful that shimmered before her, just out of reach. She moved against him, edging toward the nameless need that had taken over her whole being. And finally she touched it.

Her mouth opened on a soundless cry and she arched up as her orgasm washed over her. Her internal muscles pulsed around his finger in waves of endless pleasure that seemed to go on and on.

When it was over she was self-conscious again, where before she'd been so lost in her pleasure that she hadn't really stopped to realize that she should be embarrassed about what he was doing to her.

"Don't," he said, deftly undoing the buttons on his shirt.

"Don't?"

"Don't be embarrassed." He shrugged the shirt off then removed his pants and underwear in one fluid movement.

She could only stare, openmouthed at the vision of masculine perfection he'd unveiled. That muscular chest was bare for her again and she ached to touch him, to taste him. And then her gaze dropped to his erection, thick and fully aroused, and she forgot her embarrassment. How could she be embarrassed when she could see for herself how much he'd enjoyed doing that for her? When she could see how much he wanted her still? Men couldn't fake a reaction like that, and she couldn't help but feel an immense amount of feminine pride over his obvious desire for her.

He stood up from the bed and moved over to the dresser where there were several pillar candles set out. She took the opportunity to admire his tight male butt, her arousal almost unbearable despite the orgasm she'd just had. He grabbed a lighter from the top drawer and picked up one of the candles.

"What are you doing?" she asked, craving his skin against hers, craving his touch, his kiss.

"Setting the mood," he said, the corner of his mouth lifting into a smile.

"There's no time for that," she said, shimmying out of her dress. "I need you. Now."

A feral growl rose up in his throat and he crossed to the bed in three quick strides. Then he was covering her, gently pressing her legs apart with his hair-roughened thigh. She kissed him, moved against him, rubbed her breasts against his chest. She loved being naked with him, skin to skin, their bodies twined together. It was the most amazing feeling in the world. She was completely out of control, and yet she was safe. With him she was safe. No matter what. She knew it instinctively, even if she didn't know why.

He rubbed his shaft against her slick opening. She was so wet, so ready for him after her first mind-numbing orgasm that she didn't feel any pain when he started to ease into her. She opened her eyes and looked at him. His face was tense, the tendons in his neck strained with the concentration it took for him to go slow.

She looped her calf over his and urged him on. In one quick motion he thrust inside of her to the hilt. She felt too full, the stretching sensation uncomfortable, but not painful. She shifted, trying to ease some of the pressure.

He pulled away and then pushed into her again and she felt her body adjusting, felt her muscles expanding to accommodate him. And when he thrust into her for a third time all of the discomfort was gone. She moaned with pleasure, the sweet feeling of impending orgasm beginning to coil in her pelvis again.

"Oh, Max," she breathed, arching against him, meeting each of his thrusts.

He buried his face in her neck, his movements wild, hard. Wonderful. Neither of them were quiet, both of them whispering words of encouragement, letting the other one know how good everything was. And when she felt ready to go over the edge again she jumped willingly.

If her first orgasm was a release, this one was an explosion of feeling. She couldn't stop the hoarse cry that escaped her lips as she lost herself in her own pleasure wholly and completely. He thrust hard into her one last time and pressed a hot kiss to her lips as he came.

He held her until their raging heartbeats calmed, their bodies still joined.

"I didn't know," she said, dazed. "I didn't know that losing control could be so...empowering."

His lips twitched against her neck. "Was it?"

"Yes. I didn't know it could be like that."

"Was it your first orgasm?" he asked, surprise lacing his voice.

She hadn't planned on telling him, but after that she knew there was no place for lying or even sidestepping the truth. "Yes. My first everything."

Max was stunned by that admission. She'd been tight, so tight it had been a battle not to come the moment he'd thrust into her, but he'd been too lost in his own pleasure to question it.

"And why is that, Alison? You're a beautiful woman. A sensual woman. There wouldn't have been anything wrong with you exploring that."

"Control," she said softly. "I never wanted to give

anyone the power to hurt me. So I avoided relationships. Avoided sex."

"What made you change your mind?"

She shifted in his arms and turned to face him, her copper eyes still cloudy with the aftereffects of her orgasm. Something that felt a lot like pride swelled in his chest. "You're the first man that I wanted to be with. Before I... It scared me to think of being with someone like this. Being naked, not just physically, but in every way. But I trust you. I trust that you won't hurt me," she said simply.

He felt as if a steel band was clamping down hard on his heart. She'd been a virgin. She'd trusted him where she hadn't trusted any man before. And what could he offer her but a cold, clinical relationship, void of any kind of sentimental emotion. She deserved more than that. But he just didn't have it in him.

"I can't give you love. I can't give you the promises a woman should expect after her first time."

"I don't need any more promises. And we're already engaged," she said pointedly. "And what we have is better than love. We have honesty. We have a common bond. "

She was right. Love was no guarantee of anything, and they'd both seen that firsthand in life. He only hoped she wouldn't have a change of heart. Virgins tended to take sex very seriously, which was why he'd always avoided them.

She slid her silky smooth thigh over his and her damp core brushed against his penis. He felt himself getting hard all over again. He wanted her. Already. Wanted her so badly his muscles were knotting with tension as he tried to hold himself back. But she'd been a virgin less than a half hour ago and he wasn't going to hurt her by trying to find his own satisfaction again so soon.

She moaned and moved against him, her lips curved into a dreamy smile.

"Alison," he bit out. "Be careful."

"Why?" she asked, a full-blown smile spreading over her face. He found himself smiling back.

"Because you're new at this and I don't want to hurt you."

"You didn't hurt me at all the first time."

"But I can't promise I'll behave myself this time. It's been a very long time for me."

Her eyes widened. "It has?"

"I haven't been with a woman since before Selena died."

The stricken look on her face made his gut tighten. "Was this…? I mean…you don't feel guilty, you don't feel like…?"

"Do I feel like I betrayed my wife?"

She nodded. "Yes."

"No. It wasn't about that. There was no woman that I wanted to be with. I'd dated casually and I had put that behind me. I was married for seven years and I still wanted the stability it offered. Yet I didn't want to get married again, either. That didn't leave me with a lot of options."

"And then you got stuck with me," she said, her smile sad now.

He shifted to his side and propped himself up on his elbow. "I didn't want to get married again because my marriage was such a disaster in the end," he said, finally saying what he'd never before voiced out loud. "Selena and I no longer shared a bed, or much of anything else. There was no way for me to reach her anymore, and I stopped trying. Then she was killed in the car accident while I was away on business. I wasn't even there to hold her hand while she died. It was my job to protect her, and I didn't."

"Oh, Max." She buried her face in his chest as he cupped the back of her head, stroking her hair. "You couldn't have protected her from that."

"I should have been there for her. At the very least I could have done that. I could have tried harder to make her happy."

"If she wouldn't talk to you there was nothing you could do to make her. She chose not to share with you."

"One person cannot bear all the blame when a marriage dissolves. She was fragile, and life forced her to endure things that would have wounded a much stronger person. I had a duty to my wife that I didn't fulfill."

Her expression turned fierce, a golden spark lighting her eyes. She put her hand on his cheek. "We have a duty to each other, Max. To make this work. I promise I'll never close up like that on you. I won't freeze you out. We'll always talk."

He kissed her softly on the corner of her lips, then more firmly as he rolled her underneath him. The feeling that swelled in his chest when she made that promise was far too much, far too intense. It shouldn't matter. His relationship with Alison was about passion, and their baby. Nothing more. Emotions simply didn't enter the equation.

But that simple vow kept pounding through him as he made love to her, fueled his desire for her. And when she cried out his name during her orgasm it pulled feelings from his hardened heart that he'd no longer imagined himself capable of.

# CHAPTER TEN

"YOUR belly is starting to show." Maximo put his arms around Alison from behind and caressed her bare mid-section. She had been examining herself in the mirror in the master suite, sucking in her expanding stomach.

She swatted at his hand. "Just what every woman wants to hear!"

"It's sexy." He nuzzled her neck and kissed the hollow just beneath her ear. "You must know how sexy I think you are."

She knew. Maximo had spent all night showing her just how sexy he thought she was. It had been a revelation. She'd discovered a whole, huge part of herself she hadn't even known existed. A part of herself she'd spent far too long suppressing. She'd given her control over to Maximo for a while, and it had been freeing in a way she'd never imagined it could be. And now that they were out of bed she had her control back, and her heart was still intact. She could do this. She could maintain her independence and have a relationship with him. She wasn't going to love him, or need him in any way beyond the physical.

"The feeling is definitely mutual." She turned and wound her arms around his neck and traced his squared jaw with her fingertip. A tidal wave of possessiveness crashed over her. He was so very handsome. And he was hers. "I'm going to hold you to that forsaking all others bit in the marriage vows."

"I will keep my vows, Alison. Why take them otherwise?"

"Millions of people make the same vows all the time. It doesn't guarantee the promise will be kept."

"It may surprise you to know that I'm familiar with the issues people face in marriage."

She winced. "Sorry, but I told you I'd talk to you if I had issues. I just wanted to let you know I was feeling possessive."

He offered her a tight smile. "I appreciate that. Maybe if Selena had talked to me we wouldn't have grown so far apart." He moved away from her and walked to the closet, pulling out a T-shirt and shrugging it over his head. "Of course, even saving our marriage wouldn't have changed anything in the end."

"You couldn't have saved her if you were there, Max. It was an accident. It wouldn't have changed anything. You did what you could in your marriage. It isn't your fault that she wouldn't talk to you."

He shook his head. "She depended on me. I should have tried harder. Instead I got frustrated. I worked more. I should warn you that I'm not a very good husband. I'm not good at reading emotions. I travel a lot. I get absorbed with my business."

She put her hand on his arm. "You're a good man, Maximo. You're going to be a good husband, and a wonderful father. In my line of work I've dissolved more marriages than I care to think about, and then, at the Children's Advocacy Center I saw a lot of men who were lousy husbands *and* fathers. You're not like them."

"You say that, Alison, and I think you even mean it,

but you've only known me for three weeks. Selena had seven years to grow disenchanted with me."

"I think all marriages can lose their luster if you let them," she said firmly. "But we're getting married for a reason."

"The baby." He put his hands over her rounded belly and rested her palm over them.

"Yes. That reason is never going to go away. We'll always have our child in common."

"And that's enough for you?"

She gave him a level stare, her eyes never wavering from his. "It has to be, doesn't it?"

He nodded firmly. Decidedly. "Yes."

"Then it is. We're going to make this work for our child. We're going to make a family. That's all that matters. When I make my vows I'll keep them."

Maximo ignored the tightening sensation in his chest. Ignored the voice in his head berating him for allowing this woman to settle for so much less than she deserved. "Then you would be in the minority."

She shrugged one delicate shoulder. "I'm used to that by now. I was a twenty-eight-year-old virgin until last night, remember?" She gave him a sly grin.

"How could I forget?"

"I don't know. Perhaps you need your memory refreshed." And then she was in his arms, stroking his back with her hands and practically purring.

This was enough. Enough for both of them. He would do everything in his power to make it enough.

"Alison?" He cupped her bare hip bone with his hands and did wicked things to the indent that led from there to her femininity.

"Hmm?" she half moaned.

"I want to show you something."

"You already did that—" she snuggled into him "—twice," she added playfully.

"Not that."

She sighed. "I suppose we have to get out of bed at some point."

"It is advised."

They had spent most of the morning in bed and it was late afternoon now. Alison was languid, satisfied in a way, but far from sated. There would never be a time when she wouldn't crave the way Max made her feel. When he kissed her, caressed her, entered her, she felt complete.

"All right, but you have to feed the baby and me first."

"I wouldn't dream of being neglectful."

He made good on his promise and fed her lunch—a creamy pasta dish that made her very happy. Now that her morning sickness had passed she found she was loving food again, more than usual even. After she was finished, Max took her hand and led her out of the villa and into the courtyard.

"Why do I get the feeling I'm being led astray?" she asked, the wicked grin on his face making her stomach flutter.

"I have no idea. I promise you my intentions are entirely pure."

"Somehow, I very much doubt that there's anything pure in your mind except for purely naughty thoughts."

He laughed and the sound made her heart jump in her chest. "No. You'll see."

There was a small whitewashed building that rested on an outcrop of rock that overlooked the beach below.

It seemed as though it was nearly carved into the cliff, a part of nature. It had obviously been built years earlier than the villa, the mature, creeping vines that covered the side attesting to that fact.

"This is lovely," she said.

"It's one of the reasons I picked this location to build the villa. The natural lighting inside the studio is amazing." He took a key out of his jeans pocket and put it into the ancient keyhole.

Alison was surprised by the renovation that had been done to the inside, which was light and airy, modern.

"There's a bedroom and bathroom through there." He pointed through the galley-style kitchenette and to a door that stood closed. There was sparse furniture in the main room, a couch, an easel and paintings lining the walls, all beautifully, photo-realistically done.

"Max…you did these, didn't you?" She could see it in each brushstroke, so controlled, so carefully placed. Maximo captured the essence of what he painted, kept the life that possessed his subject in the real world and translated it to the canvas. It didn't possess the freedom of expression, the broad, abstract work of a modern artist, but it wouldn't have been Max if it had.

"Yes."

"Does anyone know?"

He shook his dark head and came to stand close behind her. "It's something I've dabbled in over the years, but never devoted much time to."

"That's a crime! Max, these are beautiful!" She moved up close to a landscape portrait of the waves crashing on the rocks. It was the view out the window it was placed next to, and it rivaled the real thing. The water was alive and the wind was a living thing, too, moving the grass in a sea of green ripples.

"It isn't what's popular. I invest in art. I wouldn't invest in these. They're the kind of pictures that hang in a doctor's office."

"They're amazing." She reached a hand out, letting it hover over the exquisite work. "Do you only do landscapes?"

"So far. As I said, I haven't had much time to devote to it."

"Selena never saw them?" she asked gently, watching his eyes darken with stormy emotion.

"No." Just no. No explanation. She didn't need one. Selena had not loved the man standing before her. She may have loved the idea of him. The powerful, handsome prince with the gorgeous body and amazing bedroom skills. But she hadn't loved *him*. He was so much more than what he chose to show the world. And she had been blessed with a window into his heart.

"I'm honored that you showed me."

He turned to her. "I want to paint you."

"Me?"

He laughed. "Yes. I have never done a portrait. I haven't been inspired to. But I want to paint you."

This was more intimate for him, she realized, than making love. He was sharing something with her that he had not shared with any other woman, any other person, period. That did something to her. It made the most bittersweet pain twist her heart, made her stomach tighten with longing.

"I would like that."

He put an arm around her and took her chin in his hand, tilting her face up so that their eyes met. "I want to paint all of you."

Realization of what that meant dawned slowly. "I can't do that!" she protested, her cheeks heating at the idea of getting naked in such bright daylight and lying exposed for hours on end.

"I'm realizing that you're the kind of woman who can do anything she decides to do, and heaven help the man who stands in your way. But I wouldn't want you to be uncomfortable."

She bit her lip. Still unsure.

"Have I ever done anything to hurt you? Disrespect you?" he asked gently. She shook her head. "And I never will."

She nodded slowly. And she realized that in this moment he would be as bare as she was. Because this was a part of himself he'd never shared before. And he was exposing it to her, revealing himself. And she wanted to do the same.

"I trust you." She pushed the top button of her blouse through the loop and separated the fabric that concealed her body from him. Then the next one. And the next. And on to every other piece of clothing until she was standing bare in front of him. She fought the urge to cover up. It was different during lovemaking. He was so busy kissing and touching her, he wasn't simply *staring* at her. And she was never fully conscious enough to be embarrassed of her body during sex. But now she was acutely aware of the fact that her stomach was no longer flat and that her breasts had only grown more voluptuous, along with her hips. And he wanted to capture it eternally on canvas.

She felt her whole body flush. "I'm not beautiful like…"

"Don't say you're not beautiful. And don't ever compare yourself to other women. You're *my* woman. And I happen to find you exquisitely beautiful."

She thrilled at the raw, masculine possession that

laced his voice. She should find him arrogant, or at least sexist. She couldn't.

Maximo could barely keep his desire leashed. She was so enchanting, pale and vulnerable, in the midafternoon sunlight that filtered in through the picture window, when she was normally so strong, wearing her independence like armor. The artist in him longed to paint her; the man in him simply wanted to make love to her until neither of them could think or move.

He settled for picking up a sketch pad and a clutch pencil. "Sit on the couch."

She backed away from him and lowered herself onto the chaise-style couch, reclining. She rested her head on the gentle slope of the armrest and put one arm high above her head, raising her plump breasts.

He wanted to capture everything, every curve, every line. The dent in her sweet lips, the pout in her nipples, the perfect V at the juncture of her thighs... Mostly he wanted the molten fire in her golden eyes to translate to the canvas.

Her body, tense at first, began to relax as he began to sketch. His hand moved fluidly, shaping her curves, shading the dips and hollows of her body. He drew the fullness of her breasts and ached to cup them. She arched her back as though she knew what portion of her body he was stroking with the pencil, as though she knew and wanted his touch as badly as he wanted to touch her. His body hardened painfully.

He added her small waist, her soft belly, the small bump where their baby sat. He moved lower and she gasped, her pulse pounding at the base of her neck. She moaned softly as he traced the outline of her sex on the paper. She pressed her legs together and slid her foot up her smooth thigh as he continued his study of her, as he continued to capture her forever.

A throaty growl escaped her throat. "Max." It was a plea, and it was one she didn't need to make twice.

He placed his notebook on the table and joined her on the chaise. Her hands were on him, pulling his shirt over his head, fumbling with the closure of his pants.

"What is it that you do to me?" he growled, moving his hand over her curves, tracing them as he had just done with a pencil. This was much more satisfying; flesh on flesh instead of lead on paper.

He kissed her neck, nibbling the tender flesh of her throat. "I hope it's the same thing that you do to me."

"Without a doubt it is." He shoved his jeans down along with his underwear, and relished the sensation of her hot skin against his. "I think this is going to be fast."

She gripped his buttocks with her hands and looked him in the eye. "Good. I don't think I could handle slow."

He positioned himself and sank into her tight, wet heat. He had to grit his teeth to keep from exploding then and there. It took all of his strength to stay still, to keep it from ending without her reaching satisfaction, too.

He had never felt this, this overwhelming desperation to claim a woman, to make her his, to lose himself inside of her body. Before Alison it had been years since he'd been with a woman. But this was about much more than prolonged, willful abstinence. This was something more…something unfamiliar, something that seemed to have taken on a life of its own.

His self-control snapped. He moved uncontrollably, pounding into her. She pulled her knees back so he could thrust harder, deeper. The only sound was their labored breathing and the slap of flesh meeting flesh. There was nothing gentle about their coming together. It was fire and brimstone, passion and torture. She cried his name out as she came and he followed, pumping into her, releasing everything he had into her body.

She kissed his neck, a smile curving her lips. "You're amazing, do you know that?"

He had no idea what he'd done to earn the trust he heard in her voice, and he wasn't sure he wanted it. Wasn't sure that he could fulfill all of the hopes that he saw shimmering in the depths of her beautiful eyes.

They lay in silence for a long time and he was content to simply move his hands over her curves. A small sigh escaped her lips and he wanted to understand it. And he suddenly realized he wanted to know more than that. He wanted to know everything about her, who she was and why. He couldn't recall ever feeling that need before, not concerning anyone.

"Tell me about your sister," he said, not sure why it suddenly seemed important to know.

"She was my best friend." Alison burrowed against him. "She never let having Cystic Fibrosis affect who she was. She was always smiling, even when she was sick. Kimberly was the glue for our family. When she was gone everything fell apart. My parents fell apart."

"How old were you?"

"I was twelve when she died."

"They didn't have any right to fall apart, not when you needed them," he said.

"No argument from me. But my dad just couldn't stay anymore. I don't think he could walk in the house, or look at us without remembering. And that just left Mom and me."

"And she didn't look after you, either?"

"She had enough trouble dealing with her own issues. She depended on my father. She needed him for everything. Without him, she had no security and she just… It never pays to lean on someone so much because one day they might just be gone. But then, you know all about that."

"I do," he said slowly. "But I didn't depend on Selena. She depended on me. I wasn't there for her, and because of that she had to live the last month of her life completely unhappy."

"That's not fair, Max. If you could have done something to fix Selena then I could have fixed my parents."

He let silence stretch between them. There was no point debating with her. She had been a child, while he had been an adult man, Selena's husband. And she'd been hurting, spiraling into depression, and he hadn't even realized it. Not truly. She'd said she hadn't wanted to talk, and at that point he'd been so tired of trying that he'd simply accepted it.

Alison ran her soft hand over his abs, and his stomach tightened, his whole body aching, ready for her again. If it was only his body that was affected it wouldn't be so dangerous, but his chest felt too full when he looked at her, when he touched her. It was too much. It wasn't what this was supposed to be about.

He thought about what his father had said. About the paternity test. Alison had even commented that if they'd made a mix-up at the lab in the first place, it was possible they had made a mistake and that he wasn't the father.

If that were true she would be free to go back home. They wouldn't even have to get married.

He'd imagined that thought might make him feel

free, that the prospect of escaping marriage might make the tightness in his chest lessen. Instead it sent an intense pain shooting through him, targeting his heart. It shouldn't hurt like that to think of her leaving.

"We should have a paternity test done," he said firmly. "Just in case. Like you said, they made one mistake, they might have made more."

Her sweet little body that had been so soft and pliant against him went rigid in his embrace. "If you think it's necessary."

"It would be responsible."

She paused for a long moment and he could feel her drawing in short, shallow breaths. "Is there a way to do it without risk to the baby?"

"I'll find out."

"Okay." She didn't move away from him, but she wasn't melted into him anymore, either.

"We're going home tomorrow," he said, tightening his hold on her and tracing circles over the bare skin of her arm. "I need to get back and deal with some issues with one of the larger casinos."

"Okay." The note of sadness in her voice hit him like a punch in the gut. He'd upset her. He'd hurt her.

"You're disappointed?"

He felt the shrug of her slight shoulders. "This has been wonderful. But it's kind of like a fantasy. Tomorrow we're going back to reality."

"You prefer the fantasy?"

"Well, it was a wonderful fantasy."

He looked around his studio, the place he'd never shown another living soul. "Yes, it was."

After their return to Turan, Maximo's work schedule kept him away from the *castillo* during the day. He was hands-on with his work, something she greatly respected, but, despite the fact that she was keeping busy by helping to establish a Turani branch of the Cystic Fibrosis Foundation, she missed him horribly while she rattled around the huge castle.

Isabella was a cheerful, fun presence in her life, but she was busy studying her college tele-courses, and in her spare time her parents were practically keeping her under lock and key since their shopping escapade.

But even though Maximo was gone during the day, the nights were theirs. That part of the fantasy, at least, was still intact. Her passion for him hadn't ebbed, and it didn't seem as if his had for her. It was a strange thing, going from giving sex no more than the random, cursory thought, to having it be so much a part of her. Her long-denied sexuality was definitely no longer repressed, and honestly, she was happy about that. She felt more like a whole person, a whole woman, rather than someone who had a host of private hang-ups and issues that were so wound up around her she had to find an alternative way to function.

She spent every night in Max's bed, in his arms. But she kept her own room, kept her clothes hanging in the closet there, kept her makeup case in the bathroom that adjoined it, because she just wasn't ready to have everything in her life melded together with Max's. It would be too much like depending on him, and the very thought of that made her chest feel tight with panic. The wedding was in two weeks and she expected him to want her to move into his room fully after that, but until then she was retaining some sort of independence.

He was already getting under her skin, and if she wasn't careful he was going to get into her heart, too.

She sighed and checked the time on her cell phone.

Max's personal physician, Dr. Sexy, was due any minute to draw her blood for the noninvasive paternity test. And Max wasn't there. Alison clutched her orange juice, her sugar boost and last line of defense against passing out when the doctor drew the blood. She was trying not to be emotional about Max's absence, but she was pregnant and more than a little hormonal so she was finding it difficult to keep tears from welling up.

When Max had asked for the paternity test her heart had felt as if it was splintering. It had become easy to forget that they didn't have a real relationship. That their baby had been conceived in a lab. His demand for the test had been a stark reminder.

The worst thing was that she wasn't certain which result Max was hoping for.

When the beautiful doctor arrived it only took a few minutes to collect her blood sample. "All done. And we have the buccal swab from Prince Rossi already, so there really isn't anything more we need. This is a relatively new way to test paternity," she said. "If there isn't sufficient fetal DNA in your blood stream we won't get a result. But if there is then the results are just as accurate as CVS or amniocentesis."

Alison nodded, feeling the first stab of anxiety over what the test results might be.

The other woman offered her a sly smile. "Well, good luck. I know if it were me I would really be hoping it was the prince's baby. He's incredibly handsome, and of course he's wealthy enough to take care of you."

Alison shook her head. "It…it isn't like that."

She was treated to a raised eyebrow. "I only know of one reason to test for paternity. But then, what do I know? I'm just a doctor."

Alison's hand itched to do something very out of

character and very hormonal and slap the smug smile right off the other woman's face. But just a few moments later she'd collected all of her things, and with a promise to call within the next twenty-four hours she left Alison by herself again.

She collapsed into Max's plush office chair and tried to fight the tears that were seriously threatening to spill over. She'd wanted him here for this, needed him, despite her best efforts not to. Not even keeping her clothes confined to their own closet had been able to save her from it.

Cradling her face in her hands, she rested her elbows on his desk and let herself wallow in her pain. It wouldn't hurt to just give in for a while. A tear slid down her cheek and she wiped it away, annoyed at herself for crying. If she'd never found out about Max she would have done all of her testing alone, so it was just stupid to cry because he'd missed the test. But he was the one who'd wanted it, and then he hadn't even bothered to show up for it.

She lifted her head when the door to the office opened. Her pulse jumped when Maximo walked in. Even when she was mad at him he still had the most powerful effect on her body. On her heart.

"You missed the test," she said, swiping at the remaining moisture on her cheeks.

"What happened?" he asked, his expression tight.

"Nothing. She came and drew my blood. She'll tell us the results within twenty-four hours."

"Then why are you crying?"

She sucked in a deep breath. "I wanted you here."

"Why? We won't have the results until tomorrow? Why did you want me here for the blood draw?"

"I…" The words stuck in her throat. "I needed you."

His eyes darkened. "I thought you didn't do need."

"Well, I don't usually, but I needed you for this."

He set his laptop case hard on his desk, his body radiating tension. "I told you that my work keeps me away. I may be royalty, but contrary to what you might think about royals, I have duties to attend. I don't have less responsibility because I'm a prince…I have more."

"This isn't about general neediness," she said, standing up and planting her hands on her hips. "I wanted some support for a paternity test, which *you* demanded, by the way. I don't think that's very outrageous."

"I don't have time to deal with temper tantrums." His clipped words hung in the silence of the room and she let them, let herself absorb how much they hurt.

She brushed past him and out of the office, her heart feeling as if it was cracking to pieces inside of her. She didn't know how she'd let this happen. But sometime in the past six weeks she'd done what she'd vowed she would never do. She'd started needing someone. And worse than that, she was almost certain that she loved him, too.

# CHAPTER ELEVEN

ALISON was more than thankful for having an opportunity to get out of the palace later that day. The meeting with the men and women she was working with to organize the Turani branch of the CF Foundation had gone well. And it had provided some much-needed distraction from the anxiety of waiting for the test results, from the stifling solitude that came from being in a huge building surrounded by people who basically never talked to her. But most of all, she needed a distraction from her earlier revelation.

She didn't want to love Maximo. She was saving her love for her child. She didn't want to have her emotions tangled up in loving him, not when he was only going to hurt her. She didn't want to be like her parents. Didn't want to become a bitter, angry person simply because her strongest emotions had been tied up in someone who neither wanted, nor deserved them.

She hiked her purse up higher on her shoulder, clinging to the leather strap as if it might offer her some kind of support. How had she let Maximo come to mean so much to her? He was infuriating. He always thought he was right and he was ridiculously self-confident. And he was handsome. Smart. Funny. A great conversationalist. And great in bed.

She sighed audibly. She couldn't even list his sins without turning sappy. And lustful. Even now, when she was furious at him, she wanted him. The mental count-down to when she would be able to see him tonight had already begun, and she was more than a little ashamed to admit that.

"Excuse me, miss."

Alison turned her head sharply to follow the sound of the person who'd spoken to her and a flash went off in her face. Putting her head down she walked faster, her face set into the most hostile expression she could manage. She wasn't about to be intimidated by an idiot reporter, and she certainly wasn't going to stop and answer questions.

"Miss Whitman, is it true you recently underwent a paternity test?" A second voice, a woman's, joined the first.

Alison's heart jolted. They knew about the baby. About the test. She doubted it was the doctor who'd told. The position of private physician to royalty prob-ably paid way too much to betray confidences. A lab tech, though, might be tempted. However it happened, the news was out and she'd have to deal with it as best she could.

The jostle of equipment behind her grew louder and more questions, by more people, starting swirling around her.

"Is it the prince's baby?"

"Who's the father?"

"How many men are being tested?"

She bit her lip to contain an onslaught of angry words. She wasn't going to turn around and freak out at all of the people holding cameras. That photo was not going on the front page of a tabloid.

The knot of people caught up to her and suddenly she was in the middle of them, cameras and tape recorders being shoved at her from every direction. One of the men got pushed into her and she wobbled, losing her balance and falling onto the sidewalk.

That didn't seem to bother any of the rabid paparazzi. They continued to snap pictures and shout anything to get a response from her, questions, accusations.

"Alison?"

She recognized Maximo's voice over the din that surrounded her. One of the reporters who'd been leaning over her jerked back sharply, a look of shock on his face. Then she saw Max. He reached down and took her hand, pulling her gently to her feet. The reporters weren't at all deterred by his presence and they continued to crowd in.

One of the men physically grabbed Alison's arm in an attempt to slow her down. A feral growl escaped Maximo's lips and he released his hold on Alison, grabbing the man's camera and smashing it against the side of one of the brick buildings that lined the sidewalk.

"Do not lay a hand on my woman," Max gritted, his voice fierce, his normally subtle accent thick.

The photographer paled and fell back, as did the rest of them, obviously sensing impending violence if they continued their assault.

"Get in the car." Max didn't have any tenderness for her, either. He jerked open the passenger door of the black sports car that was parked against the curb.

She wasn't exactly thrilled at the thought of being in an enclosed space with him in his current mood, but she'd rather take her chances with him than have him leave her with the pseudopress. She got in and buckled up quickly.

Maximo didn't speak the entire drive back to the palace. He sat straight, gripping the steering wheel, his jaw locked tight, tension radiating off him. And she wasn't going to be the one to break that silence, not when she knew any words coming from him were going to be extremely unpleasant.

As soon as they were closed into his bedroom he unleashed his rage. "What were you thinking? You didn't tell me where you were going, you didn't take a bodyguard. I had to find out by calling your driver and he informed me you were at a meeting. Alone. That was incredibly irresponsible of you."

"Irresponsible?" she shot back. "I was trying to keep busy, trying to do something worthwhile. I am not going to sit around the castle by myself until you need me to be your royal accessory!"

"I never said that I expected you to that, but I do expect you to possess some modicum of sense." He grabbed her arm and pulled her to him, bringing her tight against his chest. "Do you have any idea what might have happened to you?"

Maximo took a sharp breath. Anger and panic roared through him, mingling with the fierce pumping of adrenaline in his veins. She affected him far too much. He had been there. He'd tried love and marriage. It had been hell. Losing Selena by increments, and finally to death, had been an exercise in torture. He had no desire to go back to that, to ever feel that way again.

When he'd seen Alison on the ground with that pack of wolves surrounding her…it had taken all of his self-control to stop himself from beating the man who'd touched her until he was unconscious. In that moment, seeing the paparazzi around her…it had been a return to the darkest moments of his life. He'd been able to imagine far too clearly what it would be like to lose her, to lose the baby. It had felt as though his world was caving in. She was starting to matter far too much, this whole tentative future with a wife and child was starting to mean too much. He had let it all go before, had had no choice but to give up on that desire. And now it had become the center of everything again. He had not intended for that to be the case.

It had seemed a simple task to keep her at arm's length. And she'd seemed more than happy to hold herself separate from him. He'd thought he could exorcize the intense passion he felt for her by making love with her, and yet every night his need for her only seemed stronger.

He'd loved Selena, but he had been in control of that love. She'd needed him, had looked to him for her everything, for comfort, for strength. That had been a role he was comfortable with then. He'd liked that she'd depended on him.

But Alison had burrowed beneath his skin. She had made herself important to him, essential in so many ways.

"Nothing was going to happen to me!" she protested.

"They knocked you over and still their only thought was getting the dirt on you, on us, digging up whatever scandal they possibly could. The night Selena was killed, they'd been following her. After the accident they took pictures," he spat. "They wanted to know if she was drunk, or on drugs. They wanted scandal."

Alison's face paled. "I never knew. It was never in the paper…it didn't…"

"I paid them off," he said, his voice low. "There was

no scandal anyway, but I feared they might publish the pictures. I bought them and had them destroyed."

Her eyes filled with tears, for him, for Selena. It rocked him, made his heart seize and his chest ache. She cupped his face and kissed him tenderly, her lips soft against his.

"I'm so sorry," she whispered.

He wanted to pull away, to leave so that he could gather his thoughts, regain control. But he couldn't leave, not with her standing there, looking devastated and vulnerable and so beautiful she made his hands shake with desire for her. He cupped her chin and tilted her face up, kissing the streaks her tears had tracked on her lovely face.

His heart thundering in his chest, he began to release the buttons on her silk blouse, baring her demure lace bra. He swallowed, nearly undone by the fierce desire rocketing through him. But it was more than that, more than just physical need. He had never felt anything like this before, not with Selena, not with any woman. He felt incomplete unless he was touching her, kissing her, stroking her gorgeous body.

His mind rejected that thought even as his heart, his body, ached to be joined with her. He could not allow her to matter so much. He had loved Selena, but she had not touched him in this way, had not wielded this kind of power over his body and his emotions. And still, when he'd lost her it had felt as though his world had crumbled.

Alison meant far more to him. In that moment when he'd thought she might have been hurt he had been able to imagine losing her. It had been like staring into a dark void that was opening up, preparing to swallow him whole, leaving him with nothing but eternal blackness. He could not allow that. But he couldn't stop kissing her.

He growled roughly and tightened his hold on her, kissing her hard, bruising her lips with the force of his passion, his rage. It was a kiss designed to punish her for what she made him feel, designed to reassert his dominance. He plundered her mouth, dipping his tongue deep inside before nipping the fullness of her bottom lip.

When he parted from her, her eyes were huge, her breathing ragged. Her nipples were beaded, pressed against the flimsy bra. She wanted him still, even though she'd been angry with him. And God help him, he wanted her.

He denied the refrain that was playing through his mind, denied the insistent tattoo of her name that was beating through him. It wasn't about her. She wasn't special. She was just a woman. And he was a man. He wanted what a man desired of a woman and nothing more. It wasn't Alison; it was just sex. He had been without it for too long; that was why she affected him so strongly.

He backed her across the room and turned her so that she was facing away from him before bending her gently over the surface of the dresser that was positioned up against the wall.

"Max?" she asked tremulously.

"Trust me," he grated.

He moved his hands up her still-slender waist, around to her stomach and over the little bump that housed their baby. His heart jumped and he curled his hands into fists before opening them again and palming her breasts, releasing the front clasp on her bra and letting it fall open. He covered the creamy mounds, squeezed her sensitized nipples, drawing a low, desperate moan from her lips.

He abandoned her breasts to push her skirt down her hips, taking her tiny pair of panties with it. He pressed his hand against her mound, pushing one finger through her slick folds and finding the bud that housed her most sensitive nerve endings. She shivered, her head falling back to rest against his chest. The sweet scent of her perfume, so uniquely her, assaulted him. He swept her hair to the side and kissed her neck, her bare shoulder.

Unsteadily he reached for the closure on his slacks and freed himself, bringing his naked flesh against the softness of her bottom. She gasped and arched into him, pressing the heart of her, her glorious wetness, up against his aching body.

Keeping one hand centered on her clitoris, stroking her mercilessly; he splayed his other hand across her stomach and tilted her back gently as he thrust into her tight heat.

He lost all sense of control, all sense of time. He had wanted to take her this way to make it impersonal, so he couldn't see her face. But he knew…her scent, the feel of her soft skin beneath his hands, the soft sounds of pleasure that she made…the fact that his body had never responded this way to any other woman. It was Alison, and he could not deny it.

He kissed the side of her neck, gentled his touch on her breasts, let his hands slide over her soft curves. His heart squeezed in his chest. This was Alison. His woman. The mother of his child. There was no denying it, and he didn't want to.

Suddenly he needed to see her, needed to watch her face as he brought her to the peak, needed to cradle her close to his body. He withdrew and swept her into his arms, crossing the room quickly and settling her onto the bed. "Alison," he whispered, brushing her hair back off her forehead.

She raised her hands and cupped his cheek, the emotion in her eyes nearly undoing him completely. "Max."

He entered her slowly, his entire body trembling with the effort to maintain control. She locked her arms around him, moved with him, her soft sighs of pleasure gratifying him in a way that went far beyond the physical. And after she had cried out her climax he rushed to follow her, and it was her name that he whispered hoarsely as he came hard, spilling himself inside her, branding her. Branding himself.

Emotion tightened his chest, squeezed down hard on his heart and refused to release him from its iron fist. The look in her eyes, the one of pure wonderment, affected him too much. He rolled away from her suddenly, pulling away from the feelings roiling inside of him.

She turned to her side, facing him, and his breath caught when the full impact of her beauty hit him. Her face was flushed, her mouth swollen. She had never looked more enticing, more lovely. He gritted his teeth against the rising tide of emotion that was threatening to swamp him.

"I have work to do." He turned away from her and buckled his belt, his breathing ragged, his heart pounding hard. His instinct was to go to her, to hold her. But he wouldn't allow himself that. Wouldn't allow himself to show that level of weakness.

He could hear her behind him, collecting her clothing, and when he turned to face her again he could read the hurt and confusion she clearly felt. He didn't have to say anything for her to know that he was distancing himself from her. That itself was enough for him to want distance. He didn't want her feelings involved any more than he wanted to involve his own.

"I'll be working late tonight. You should sleep in your own room," he said, his voice clipped.

She flinched as though he'd struck her. "Okay."

Her mobile phone rang and she reached down and fished it out of her purse, which had been thrown to the floor at some point in their frantic hurry to come together.

She checked the caller ID. "It's the lab." She answered, but neither her face nor her tone gave away any information. She hung up and focused on him, her lips pressed firmly together. "Congratulations. You're the father. We're ninety-nine-point-nine percent certain now." She didn't sound happy, she didn't look happy.

Alison watched Maximo's face, hoping for some kind of reaction, something she could hold onto to let her know that she hadn't lost him, lost everything they'd built together in the past six weeks. When he'd withdrawn from her physically she'd felt his emotional withdrawal just as keenly, could see his dark eyes flatten as he walled his emotions off from her.

"I have to go," he said, his dark eyes unreadable.

Alison tried to do what he'd done so easily, tried to block out the pain she knew was about to hit. But it was impossible. She loved him too much, and she was losing him already. He might never leave her, but she would never have his heart, either.

She pushed hard against her closed eyes, trying to stop tears from falling. She was going to be strong, for herself, for her baby. She would never let anyone know that her heart was shattered irreparably.

* * *

The fragrant air caressed her skin, the intense warmth of the summer day heating her. But only on the outside. Everything inside of her was cold.

She'd arrived on the island of Maris only twenty minutes ago, hoping she might find some solace for her pain. Instead being in the place where she had been so happy, where she had been awakened to love and making love, was a bittersweet pain. She had never felt more separate from him.

He'd been away on business more often than not over the course of the past week, and when he'd been home he'd been unfailingly polite. Distant. It was worse than his anger—at least that was passionate. He was acting like a stranger. He hadn't made love with her, not since the day she'd been attacked by the paparazzi.

That was when things had changed. When he'd shut her out completely. Her worst fear was that it wasn't related to the incident with the press, but that it had to do with him finding out for certain he was the father of her baby. Maybe he didn't want them anymore. And now, his get-out-of-jail-free card had been taken away from him.

She moved away from the balcony and reentered the room. The one she and Max had shared when they'd stayed here. She shivered. It had been a stupid idea to come to the island. But her heart was breaking, splintering with every beat it took, and she had to try to fix it somehow.

Maybe if there would have been a big blow-up fight it would have been easier. If he'd said ugly things and told her he didn't want her, maybe then her love would have died. But it had just been this sudden, silent break. He had withdrawn from her completely with no explanation, but the separation had been a no less definite or final feeling than if they had experienced some kind of dramatic end to their relationship.

The greatest irony was that their wedding was in two days. In two days they were going to stand before the congregation and make vows to love, honor and cherish each other. It would be difficult since they were barely speaking to each other.

She rested her palm on her burgeoning belly and felt renewed determination. She wasn't destitute. She had her baby, the most precious thing in the world. She loved Max. She loved him so much it actually hurt, but their baby was a piece of them. They may not have created life in the usual, physical way, but the baby was the best of both of them.

She heard footsteps behind her on the travertine floor and turned, expecting to see Rosa Maria, the housekeeper. Instead she saw Max striding toward her. He was as intimidating as ever, a man who oozed control and sophistication. But there was something different. She noticed the fatigue etched in his handsome face. She could definitely relate.

"What are you doing here, Maximo?"

He laughed, the sound hollow, void of any joy or humor. "The same thing as you, I would imagine. Trying to escape."

"What is it you need to escape from?"

He laughed again. "The same thing as you I would imagine."

"Please, Max, I'm not up to playing games with you."

"So it's Max again, is it?" His voice softened and he took a step toward her.

"What do you mean?"

He gave her a half smile. "I was demoted to the more formal Maximo."

"I didn't even realize."

"I did," he said huskily.

Her throat tightened. She couldn't take this. This tease. He didn't want her. He was stuck with her.

"Why are you here?" she asked, anguish lacing her voice.

"This is where I've been for most of the past week," he confessed.

"I thought you were working."

"In a way I was."

Frustration bubbled through her. "I don't want your passion one moment and your silence the next. I can't do hot and cold. I don't know what happened to change things between us. But you won't tell me. If I've done something then say it. If you've found someone else, or you're simply tired of me, *say it*. Don't freeze me out. Don't make me play guessing games."

"I'm not a man of words, Alison. I'm a man of actions. You may have noticed that," he said with dark humor. "I don't always say the right things. But I want the chance to make you understand me. To make you understand how I feel."

She shook her head, her throat tightening with tears. "Don't play with me."

He took her hand, and their first physical contact in a week rocked her to her core. The wanting hadn't gone away. Not even for a moment. She could see from the molten heat in his eyes that he felt the same.

"I've never been playing with you," he said, his voice intense. "Please know that. I've handled things badly, but hurting you was the last thing I wanted."

"But you did hurt me," she said. "We promised we

were going to talk about things, but we didn't. You just shut me out, and I have no idea what happened to cause it."

He raised his eyes and met hers; the stark, raw emotion in them shocked her. "I know," he said roughly. "You cannot know how sorry I am. Please come with me, Alison."

She nodded slowly and let him lead her from the villa. When she realized where they were headed she stopped. "Max. I can't."

"Trust me. Please."

She took a breath and allowed him to take her the rest of the way to the art studio, her heart a leaden weight in her chest. This was the place where she had shed her inhibitions, where she had laid herself bare to him. Where she had lost her heart. Coming here was the worst sort of torture mingled with the sweetest of memories. They had been connected then, and even though she hadn't been able to name the things he'd made her feel, it was where she'd fallen in love with him.

He opened the door and took her into the sun-bathed room. There was no question of what he had wanted her to see. It was there in the middle of the room, lit up by the incandescent natural light. It was her, but it wasn't her. The woman captured on the canvas was beautiful. Her skin glowed with youth and joy. As though she had just been with her lover and he had left her satisfied. The painting was exquisitely detailed. Her hair was a lush mix of reds and golds, her flesh palest peach, her lips and nipples a dusky rose. Her eyes were closed, her full mouth curved, hinting at secrets. Secrets between her lover and herself, because there could be no doubt that this woman was well-loved.

She looked at the painting piece by piece, something

inside of her moved by it. The features were hers, but there was something more, something she didn't see when she looked in the mirror. Something Maximo saw that she didn't see in herself. It was more than a portrait, it was a revelation. A declaration. It spoke of feelings deeper than words; it mirrored what she felt in her heart.

"Max?"

"This is what I've been doing. I wasn't working. I couldn't work. My mind was filled with you, Alison." He cupped her cheek and dropped a light kiss on her mouth. He tasted of desperation, of need, and her body responded; along with her heart.

"Max…"

"No, I have to say this. I was scared, Alison. Scared of how much you had come to mean to me. That day forced me to face what it might feel like if I were to lose you. I don't think I could survive it. I realized how much you'd come to mean to me, how much I counted on seeing you every day, kissing you, making love with you. I realized how much I needed you. I did not want you to have so much power over me. I didn't want to love you." A sad smile touched his lips. "I tried to shut you out. To prove to you, and to myself, that I didn't need you. I was very wrong."

He kissed her fiercely and she parted her lips for him, closing her eyes as she reveled in being held again by the man that she loved.

He tilted his head and rested his forehead against hers. "I have more to say, but I'm afraid I won't say it right. I need to show you first." He kissed her neck, her cheek, her forehead. "Can I show you?" he asked against her lips.

"Yes," she half sobbed, half laughed.

He lifted her shirt up over her head, exposing her sensitive breasts to his inspection. He groaned when he saw that she was bare beneath her shirt. "Oh, my darling, what you do to me." He cupped her aching flesh reverently, his thumbs moving back and forth over her distended nipples. A cry formed on her lips and he kissed it away.

She put her hands on his broad chest, touching him, tasting the salty skin at the base of his throat as though it was the first time. Everything seemed new. Fresh. She pushed his shirt up over his head and tossed it on the ground to join her rumpled blouse.

She undid the snap on his jeans, her eyes utterly transfixed on the line of hair that ran down his taught, flat belly and disappeared into his pants. She knew where it led, and yet the curiosity and excitement she felt made it seem as though she didn't.

"You're so sexy," she breathed.

With a growl he pushed her onto the couch, settling between her willing thighs. "Oh, Alison, my love, you don't know how that makes me feel. It's unlike anything else in this life."

"I think I have an idea." She opened herself to him, bring his shaft against the moist heart of her body.

He kissed her, deeply, all consuming, as though he was trying to devour her. He stripped her pants and underwear off in one fluid movement and then took care of his own, leaving them naked. No barriers. Nothing between them. It was as honest as two people could be with one another. There were no secrets between them, no way to hide anything. Not their insecurities, not the bulge of her tummy that housed their child, not the feeling of pure, sweet love, coursing between them.

She positioned herself over his body and took him

inside of her slowly, relishing the feeling of becoming one with him. She felt herself expand to accommodate him and she sighed with completion and satisfaction when he was buried in her up to the hilt.

She rose and fell, taking him in and pulling away almost completely each time. The rhythm took them over and they were both climbing together, their breathing synchronized, her body tightening, his expanding.

She locked eyes with him, felt tears starting to fall as she looked at the emotion in them. Emotion she was certain was mirrored in her own. They went over the edge together, holding each other, his arms the only thing keeping her from flying apart.

He cradled her in his arms, whispering soft, sweet words, flowing seamlessly from Italian to English.

*"Te amo,"* he said. "I love you."

"Max." Her voice was thick with emotion, her heart so full she thought it might not be able to hold all he was making her feel.

"I love you. I know I could have said it earlier, but I wanted to show you. I wanted to show you my heart, the painting. I wanted to show you my need, my desperation, by making love to you. Words are only words. By my actions I hoped to prove it to you. I have never felt anything like this before. You talked about need making people weak, and I was certainly a believer in that principle. But you were so brave, so enchanting. Your love for our child, your strength, everything about you called to me on such a deep level, and I couldn't control what I felt for you. I wanted you to the point of constant distraction. I needed you. It—" he hesitated "—it frightened me. I didn't want to love a woman so much, with such an all-consuming passion. But you gave me no choice.

I was powerless to stop myself from falling in love with you."

"I thought you didn't want the baby anymore. Or me, for that matter."

"What?"

"It started after the call from the doctor. I thought you were having second thoughts about tying yourself to me, about being a father. You didn't choose this, Max. You didn't choose me and I…"

"No, I didn't choose you. You were chosen for me. I didn't know what was best for me. I can only be thankful for divine intervention."

"Who said you weren't good with words?"

He leaned in and kissed her, his lips teasing hers softly. She sighed when they parted, absolute bliss radiating through her.

"I'm much better at other forms of communication," he said.

"Show me."

"It will be my greatest pleasure for the rest of my life."

# EPILOGUE

PRINCIPESSA Eliana Rossi came into the world with her mother's golden hair and her father's set of lungs. At least that's what Alison said.

"She's beautiful. Just like her *mamma*," he said, bending over to kiss both of his women. He had only been a father for a few hours, but they had already been the most spectacular hours of his life. His love for Alison had only deepened in the past few months. Seeing her now, holding Eliana, he felt so full of love he thought he might burst.

"She's hungry," Alison said, lowering the top of her hospital gown and helping her daughter latch to her breast. Maximo had never seen anything more wonderful.

"Let's have lots of children," he declared, utterly fascinated by the miracle in front of him.

She gave him a hard glare. "Wait until I recover before you even mention such a thing."

He grinned at her, sheepishly. "Good idea."

"Someday she's going to be the queen," Alison said softly.

"Yes," he agreed, "but for now she's just our daughter, and we'll do all we can to make sure she stays a little girl as long as possible." He looked down at the tiny pink bundle. "I'm in no hurry for her to grow up."

"You know something, Principe Maximo D'Angelo Rossi?" Her golden eyes shone with love as she looked at him, and he was concerned that his heart really might burst. "I think I love you even more today than I did yesterday."

He bent and kissed her again, savoring the taste of her sweet lips. "I feel the same way. And I think I'll love you even more tomorrow."

 **Harlequin** *Presents*

## Coming Next Month

from **Harlequin Presents® EXTRA**. Available April 12, 2011.

**#145 PICTURE OF INNOCENCE**
Jacqueline Baird
*Italian Temptation!*

**#146 THE PROUD WIFE**
Kate Walker
*Italian Temptation!*

**#147 SURF, SEA AND A SEXY STRANGER**
Heidi Rice
*One Hot Fling*

**#148 WALK ON THE WILD SIDE**
Natalie Anderson
*One Hot Fling*

---

## Coming Next Month

from **Harlequin Presents®**. Available April 26, 2011.

**#2987 JESS'S PROMISE**
Lynne Graham
*Secretly Pregnant...Conveniently Wed!*

**#2988 THE RELUCTANT DUKE**
Carole Mortimer
*The Scandalous St. Claires*

**#2989 NOT A MARRYING MAN**
Miranda Lee

**#2990 THE UNCLAIMED BABY**
Melanie Milburne
*The Sabbatini Brothers*

**#2991 A BRIDE FOR KOLOVSKY**
Carol Marinelli

**#2992 THE HIGHEST STAKES OF ALL**
Sara Craven
*The Untamed*

**Visit www.HarlequinInsideRomance.com
for more information on upcoming titles!**

HPCNM0411

# REQUEST YOUR FREE BOOKS!

## 2 FREE NOVELS PLUS
## 2 FREE GIFTS!

---

**YES!** Please send me 2 FREE Harlequin Presents® novels and my 2 FREE gifts (gifts are worth about $10). After receiving them, if I don't wish to receive any more books, I can return the shipping statement marked "cancel." If I don't cancel, I will receive 6 brand-new novels every month and be billed just $4.05 per book in the U.S. or $4.74 per book in Canada. That's a saving of at least 15% off the cover price! It's quite a bargain! Shipping and handling is just 50¢ per book in the U.S. and 75¢ per book in Canada.* I understand that accepting the 2 free books and gifts places me under no obligation to buy anything. I can always return a shipment and cancel at any time. Even if I never buy another book, the two free books and gifts are mine to keep forever.

106/306 HDN FC55

| | |
|---|---|
| Name | (PLEASE PRINT) |

| | |
|---|---|
| Address | Apt. # |

| | | |
|---|---|---|
| City | State/Prov. | Zip/Postal Code |

Signature (if under 18, a parent or guardian must sign)

### Mail to the **Reader Service:**
**IN U.S.A.:** P.O. Box 1867, Buffalo, NY 14240-1867
**IN CANADA:** P.O. Box 609, Fort Erie, Ontario L2A 5X3

Not valid for current subscribers to Harlequin Presents books.

**Are you a current subscriber to Harlequin Presents books
and want to receive the larger-print edition?
Call 1-800-873-8635 or visit www.ReaderService.com.**

* Terms and prices subject to change without notice. Prices do not include applicable taxes. Sales tax applicable in N.Y. Canadian residents will be charged applicable taxes. Offer not valid in Quebec. This offer is limited to one order per household. All orders subject to credit approval. Credit or debit balances in a customer's account(s) may be offset by any other outstanding balance owed by or to the customer. Please allow 4 to 6 weeks for delivery. Offer available while quantities last.

**Your Privacy**—The Reader Service is committed to protecting your privacy. Our Privacy Policy is available online at www.ReaderService.com or upon request from the Reader Service.

We make a portion of our mailing list available to reputable third parties that offer products we believe may interest you. If you prefer that we not exchange your name with third parties, or if you wish to clarify or modify your communication preferences, please visit us at www.ReaderService.com/consumerschoice or write to us at Reader Service Preference Service, P.O. Box 9062, Buffalo, NY 14269. Include your complete name and address.

---

*With an evil force hell-bent on destruction,
two enemies must unite to find a truth that turns
all-too-personal when passions collide.*

*Enjoy a sneak peek in Jenna Kernan's next installment
in her original* TRACKER *series, GHOST STALKER,
available in May, only from Harlequin Nocturne.*

"**W**ho are you?" he snarled.

Jessie lifted her chin. "Your better."

His smile was cold. "Such arrogance could only come from a Niyanoka."

She nodded. "Why are you here?"

"I don't know." He glanced about her room. "I asked the birds to take me to a healer."

"And they have done so. Is that *all* you asked?"

"No. To lead them away from my friends." His eyes fluttered and she saw them roll over white.

Jessie straightened, preparing to flee, but he roused himself and mastered the momentary weakness. His eyes snapped open, locking on her.

Her heart hammered as she inched back.

"Lead who away?" she whispered, suddenly afraid of the answer.

"The ghosts. Nagi sent them to attack me so I would bring them to her."

The wolf must be deranged because Nagi did not send ghosts to attack living creatures. He captured the evil ones after their death if they refused to walk the Way of Souls, forcing them to face judgment.

"Her? The healer you seek is also female?"

"Michaela. She's Niyanoka, like you. The last Seer of Souls and Nagi wants her dead."

Jessie fell back to her seat on the carpet as the possibility of this ricocheted in her brain. Could it be true?

"Why should I believe you?" But she knew why. His black aura, the part that said he had been touched by death. Only a ghost could do that. But it made no sense.

Why would Nagi hunt one of her people and why would a Skinwalker want to protect her? She had been trained from birth to hate the Skinwalkers, to consider them a threat.

His intent blue eyes pinned her. Jessie felt her mouth go dry as she considered the impossible. Could the trickster be speaking the truth? Great Mystery, what evil was this?

She stared in astonishment. There was only one way to find her answers. But she had never even met a Skinwalker before and so did not even know if they dreamed.

But if he dreamed, she would have her chance to learn the truth.

*Look for GHOST STALKER by Jenna Kernan,
available May only from Harlequin Nocturne,
wherever books and ebooks are sold.*

Fan favorite author
# TINA LEONARD
is back with
## an exciting new miniseries.

Six bachelor brothers are given a challenge—
get married, start a big family and whoever does
so first will inherit the famed Rancho Diablo.
Too bad none of these cowboys is marriage material!

> ## *Callahan Cowboys:*
> ### Catch one if you can!

**The Cowboy's Triplets** (May 2011)
**The Cowboy's Bonus Baby** (July 2011)
**The Bull Rider's Twins** (Sept 2011)
*Bonus Callahan Christmas Novella! (Nov 2011)*
**His Valentine Triplets** (Jan 2012)
**Cowboy Sam's Quadruplets** (March 2012)
**A Callahan Wedding** (May 2012)

"Not what I've heard," another firefighter said.

"Besides," Chief Featherstone said. "Mr. Dandridge says there are multiple skunks. We have no idea if they all sprayed him or if some of them didn't and are just waiting to go after the next person to stick his nose in the choir loft. Anyone want to take that chance?"

The firefighters fell silent.

"So we wait for animal control," Chief Burke said.

"Do you have any more questions?" Dad asked. "Because I'd like to transport him to the hospital." Dad looked at his watch. "The ophthalmologist will be meeting us there within the half hour."

Both chiefs nodded their approval. Dad packed his bag and hopped into the back of the ambulance. The two medics helped Mr. Dandridge in. Then they conferred briefly, and one stepped into the back of the ambulance with the patient. The other almost skipped on his way to the less odorous driver's seat. Michael and another firefighter came running up.

"Wait a sec," Michael called. "We've got his change of clothes."

The back door of the ambulance opened. Dad leaned out to take the clothes, and looked around until he spotted me.

"Meg," he said. "Your grandfather's in my car. Could you see that he gets home safely?"

"Why in the world did you bring him along?" I asked. While Grandfather was hale and hearty for someone in his nineties, I didn't think either the weather or the hour were suitable for dragging him out of his comfortable bed in my parents' guest room.

"I didn't exactly bring him," Dad said. "He heard the sirens. And when I got out to the car, he was already sitting there, ready to go. No use even trying to talk him out of coming. And once we figured out there was no fire, he decided to stay in the car and sulk."

He sounded uncharacteristically exasperated—with me, or with his headstrong father? No telling. He slammed the door and the ambulance set out, steering a careful course through the growing throng of onlookers.

"Well, that might solve the skunk removal problem," I said to the chiefs.

Chief Featherstone looked puzzled and glanced at Chief Burke as if seeking enlightenment.

"Meg's grandfather is Dr. Montgomery Blake," Chief Burke explained. "A very distinguished zoologist."

"Blake?" Chief Featherstone frowned slightly, no doubt puzzled that Dad and his father had different surnames. Since he was new in town, presumably he hadn't already heard about how Dad had been abandoned at birth, adopted, and only recently reunited with his long-lost father. Then he spoke again.

"The one you always see on Animal Planet?" he asked. "Getting bitten and peed on by exotic animals?"

"That's him," I said. "And I happen to know he's particularly fond of skunks. He likes their attitude."

"I'm glad someone does," Chief Burke said. "Could you ask him if he'll help, please?"

# Chapter 3

I took my time approaching Dad's van. I had misgivings about the whole idea of involving Grandfather in the skunk removal. Yes, he was a seasoned zoologist, but he'd also spent years filming nature documentaries. No documentary about skunks would be complete without showing how they sprayed their would-be attackers. And that was precisely what we wanted to avoid. What if Grandfather forgot, even momentarily, that there weren't any cameras rolling?

Dad had left the van running, obviously so the heat would stay on. Grandfather had reclined the front passenger seat as far as it would go and was fast asleep and snoring vigorously.

"Grandfather?" I touched his shoulder gently.

He started upright.

"What the hell is going on?" he asked. "Where's James?"

"Dad went to the hospital with his patient," I said.

"Well, take me home, then," he said. "Nothing to see here. So much for your big exciting fire. Should have stayed in bed and taken care of my cold."

"I can take you right away," I said. "Unless you feel up to helping us with a wildlife problem."

"Ah! What's the problem?" He unfastened his seatbelt and buttoned up his coat.

"Skunks. There are skunks in the church."

"Impossible."

"Impossible?" Couldn't he smell them? Oh—the head

cold. I wasn't sure whether to order him back into bed or envy him his apparent immunity to the prevailing stench.

"Or at least highly unlikely," he continued, as he reached over and pulled the seatbelt back across his body. "They'd all be asleep."

"You mean skunks hibernate?"

"No, but they sleep a lot more in the winter. Especially when it's cold. And with this much snow on the ground, they'd probably be snowed in their dens. Sleeping the weather out. Someone probably just saw a black-and-white cat." He closed his eyes and appeared to be settling back to continue his nap.

"Well, then we've got a whole cage of black-and-white cats, and at least one of them did a pretty good imitation of a skunk. Good enough to fool Mr. Dandridge into thinking he'd been sprayed in the eyes."

Grandfather opened one eye.

"Good enough to fool Dad into taking Mr. Dandridge down to the hospital to see an ophthalmologist."

Grandfather made a growling noise.

"Well, that could be, then," he said. "And they wouldn't like it if someone dragged them out of their dens in weather like this. And if you woke them up, they'd be downright peeved."

Apparently they weren't the only ones.

"So do you want to see the peeved skunks or do you want to go back to your den and sleep the weather out?"

He reached over, pulled a tissue from a box on the floor, and blew his nose. Then his eyes lit up.

"Ah, yes!" He sniffed appreciatively a few times, like a wine connoisseur assessing the bouquet of a rare vintage. "You could be right. Help me out of this wretched seat," he added, as he unfastened the seatbelt again.

I brought the seat back to its upright position and helped him down from the van. Then I turned off the engine, took the keys, locked the van, and scrambled to catch up with Grandfather, who had apparently regained his energy and was striding over to the two chiefs. I hoped he didn't hit an ice patch on the way.

"I hear you have a skunk problem," Grandfather said.

"Indeed," Chief Burke said. "I don't think you've met our new fire chief."

After a round of introductions, Chief Featherstone held up a piece of headgear that looked like a cross between an astronaut's helmet and a praying mantis's head.

"You can put this on to go inside," he said. "Can someone help Dr. Blake with the air tank?"

"'Air tank'? Nonsense," Grandfather boomed. "What do we need that for? I thought there wasn't a fire."

"There isn't, but the skunk smell's pretty overwhelming," Chief Burke said. "We thought—"

"Nonsense," Grandfather said. "I've smelled a few skunks in my time. Hasn't killed me yet. Come on; let's get inside. It's damned cold out here."

With that he began striding toward the front doors of the church.

"I should go with him," I said to Chief Burke, and took off in Grandfather's wake.

The two chiefs followed more slowly, probably because they stopped to put on their own helmets and strap oxygen tanks on their backs. Another firefighter followed in their wake with an armload of some kind of gear. The half dozen gleaming white steps leading up to the church slowed Grandfather down and we all stepped together into the vestibule. It was a large entryway decorated from floor to ceiling with evergreens, gold tinsel, and red velvet bows. Along the walls were brightly colored felt appliquéd banners that looked to be the work of the Sunday school classes, each illustrating a different beloved Christmas carol. The contrast between the beautiful Christmas decorations and the overpowering skunk odor would have been funny if I wasn't having so much trouble breathing.

Even Grandfather halted with a surprised look on his face. Evidently his head cold wasn't giving him total immunity.

"Where did you say the spraying happened?" he asked.

"In the choir loft." Chief Featherstone's voice was muffled by the breathing apparatus. He and Chief Burke looked rather insectoid, and the mechanical sound of their breathing was curiously unnerving, like sharing space with a pair of Darth Vaders.

Chief Featherstone marched across the vestibule and flung open the broad double doors into the sanctuary. As he was silhouetted in the doorway, I realized that even without the mask he was rather an odd figure, with a stout, barrel-shaped body perched on the thinnest legs I'd ever seen.

We followed him and stood just inside the doorway. I was beginning to regret hastily scampering after Grandfather without demanding that the fire chief lend me my own breathing apparatus.

The New Life sanctuary always overwhelmed me when I first walked in. Not so much because of its beauty, although the soaring expanses of light oak and whitewashed walls looked particularly elegant with all the evergreen, tinsel, and ribbon. No, it was the size that always got me—the place was so incredibly huge. The stained-glass windows wouldn't have been out of place in a medieval cathedral. And at the back of the church the choir loft, looming high over the altar, could probably fit almost as many people as the entire sanctuary of Trinity Episcopal, where Michael, the boys, and I had begun going a lot more regularly now that Mother had been elected to the vestry.

The sanctuary was also lined with the Christmas carol banners whose bright, cheerful colors contrasted strangely with the rank odor that was assaulting our noses. I wondered if the felt was absorbing the odor, and whether it would be possible to fumigate the banners.

"Up there." Chief Featherstone pointed at the choir loft, which was top-heavy with great looping ropes of ribbon-trimmed greenery.

"Pretty powerful odor to be coming from way up there." Grandfather sounded dubious.

"Unfortunately, it's not just coming from up there," Chief Featherstone said. "One of my men reported that in spraying Mr. Dandridge, the skunk or skunks also appear to have scored a direct hit on an intake duct for the air circulation system."

"That's going to be a challenge for the church, isn't it?" Grandfather said. "Well, how do we get up there?"

He struck a familiar pose: shoulders back, chin high, mouth firmly set, visibly determined to push through all obstacles. If we were filming one of his nature specials, this would be the signal that he was about to jump in the tank with the sharks, crawl into the lion's den, step out into the path of the charging elephant, grasp the rattlesnake's head, or whatever other foolhardy and camera-worthy stunt he'd come up with.

It would have looked more dramatic if he hadn't chosen to pose in front of a banner filled with several dozen cotton-ball sheep with broad black pipe-cleaner grins.

"I don't think there are enough handholds to do a free climb up there," I said. "But we could get some ropes and rappel up. Or— Wait! There's no camera crew. Why don't we just take the stairs?"

"Better yet, there's an elevator," Chief Burke said. "We installed it to make sure the less spry members of the choir could save their breath for singing."

"I'm perfectly able to climb a few steps," Grandfather began.

"And so am I," Chief Burke replied. "But since it doesn't look as if we'll be finished here any time soon, I think we should save our energy. Follow me."

He set off at a brisk pace toward the back of the church and to my relief, Grandfather followed.

The elevator was so small it could only fit two people at a time, so the fire chief and I waited below while Chief Burke and Grandfather went up. As soon as the elevator door closed, Chief Featherstone beckoned to the firefighter who had been trailing us. The firefighter handed me something. Another insectoid helmet.

"In case you change your mind when we get up there," Chief Featherstone said.

"I already have." With his help, I donned the helmet. The firefighter strapped on the attached oxygen tank and I sucked greedily at air that was gloriously free of skunk odor.

"Thanks," I said.

"I'm having another brought up," he said. "Maybe we can shove your grandfather into it before he pukes."

The elevator returned and we rode up in anxious silence. My heart was beating a little fast when the door opened to reveal ground zero of the skunk smell . . . .